Best Friends

Susan Walley

JourneyForth

Greenville, South Carolina

Best of Friends

Edited by Elisabeth Lyall

Cover and Illustrations by Christopher J. Pelicano

Greenville, South Carolina 29614

ISBN 0-89084-486-0

Printed in the United States of America

15 14 13 12 11 10 9 8 7 6 5 4

Dedicated to my mother,
with love, admiration, and gratitude for
her unceasing friendship and Biblical instruction

ACKNOWLEDGMENT

I sincerely thank Dawn Watkins for the countless hours that she has spent reading my manuscript and offering her expert advice. Without her encouragement this book would not have reached its final form.

PUBLISHER'S NOTE

Set in a quiet mid-western town, this story focuses on the conflicts that a child experiences while selecting and evaluating friends. Fifth-grader Katie Crawford thinks that she must choose between her friends when a new girl moves into the neighborhood. But the new girl, Renee, turns out to be a competitive but lonely girl who demands attention and recognition.

Almost too late, Katie realizes that she has made the mistake of choosing between "important" and "unimportant" friends. With her parents' help, she learns about forgiving and befriending those who hurt her and appreciating those who loyally defend her. But her most valuable lesson comes through her association with a mentally disabled boy, Louis Williams, who by his innocent devotion teaches Katie the true meaning of selfless friendship.

Contents

KATIE

Chapter One

Back to School

Katie Crawford plopped down on the top porch step, put her elbows on her knees, and rested her face in her hands.

It just wasn't fair. Here it was the very first day of school—her first day back from summer vacation—and she had to walk Louis Williams to school. Katie sighed. Today, when she had so much to talk about, she'd especially wanted to walk to school with Esther like she always did.

Katie's mom had said firmly that taking Louis was the right thing for Katie to do, and her father had agreed. So there was plainly no getting out of it.

Katie sighed again and stood up, just as Esther Gresham threw open the side door of her big maroon house across the street. "Hi, Katie!" Esther called. Her light blond hair blew away from her face as she ran to meet Katie.

Katie smiled at her best friend. "Hi, Esther! I thought you were never going to come."

"Did you have a good vacation?" Esther asked.

"Yeah!" Katie said, joining her on the sidewalk. "You've got to come over and see our pictures as soon as we get them back."

"Guess what?" exclaimed Esther. "There's a new girl in our class this year, and she goes to our church, and her name is Renee St. Vincent, and she has lots of toys. And she's even been on TV!" Esther stopped to catch her breath.

"Really?" said Katie, her jaw dropping. "She's been on TV?"

"Yes," said Esther. "She plays the violin, and she played it on TV when she was little. She told us so."

"When did you meet her?" Katie almost wished she hadn't gone on vacation.

"At Sunday school. She answered all of Miss Carmichael's questions, and she's never even been to our class before."

The girls began to climb the hill of Maple Lane. Old, sprawling houses with long windows and wide front porches lined their street. Oaks and maples towered over the peaked rooftops and shaded them from Minnesota's hot summer sun.

Just up the street, at the top of the hill, was the Williamses' house. It had a steel fence around the yard like the one at the elementary school. Along the fence clung leafy, thorned bushes with red roses drooping, their scarlet petals curling up on the ends.

"Oh, I almost forgot!" Katie said, stopping in the middle of the sidewalk.

"What?"

"We have to pick up Louis."

"Oh," said Esther, not sounding at all upset. "What's his mom doing?"

"She has a meeting with the school board this morning. Too bad Louis doesn't have a dad to take him to school."

"Katie!" exclaimed Esther. Louis's father had died years before.

"Well, it's just that a kid as big as Louis ought to be able to walk by himself," said Katie with a pout. "He's a lot older than us. He's twelve!"

Esther gave her a look, and Katie mumbled, "But I guess he can't help being disabled."

"Are we taking him home after school, too?" Esther asked cheerfully. She paused to smell the roses on the fence.

"Yeah," Katie said, bending over the roses too. She touched their soft petals. "What do you want to do this afternoon?"

"Mom says it's going to be hot and humid today," said Esther. "How about going to the swimming hole?"

"Good idea." Katie looked ahead to where Louis and Mrs. Williams were waiting by the gate. "Just don't tell Louis," she said in a low voice, "or he'll want to come too."

Mrs. Williams was short and round, and she had mostly gray hair mixed with a little black. The girls had always thought she looked at least eighty years old, but Katie's mom said that she was only fifty-five.

Louis was wearing jeans and a striped T-shirt. He was a stocky boy with straight, sandy-blond hair and slanting blue eyes.

"Hi, Mrs. Williams!" the girls called. "Hi, Louis."

"Hello, girls! How are you?" answered Mrs. Williams.

"Fine." Esther pushed the steel gate open so Louis could walk through.

"We're here to pick up Louis," Katie told her. She tried to make her voice sound enthusiastic like Esther's.

"Now, isn't that nice! Say 'thank you' to the girls, Louis."

"I go to school." Louis's button nose turned up as he smiled at them.

"Yes, we know," said Esther. "We're going, too."

"You go to school with me?" he asked.

"Yep," said Katie.

"Where are your sisters, Esther? Don't they walk to school with you anymore?" Mrs. Williams asked.

"No, they're in junior high this year. Anyway, they went to school early so they could see some new boy in their class."

"Yuck." Katie wrinkled her nose. "Is he that new girl's brother?"

"No, she just has an older sister," said Esther. "Her sister's really old—in high school!"

Mrs. Williams chuckled. "You'd better be going so you're not late. Be a good boy today, Louis," she said, letting him through the gate.

"This first day of school," said Louis as they walked toward the corner of Maple Lane.

"It sure is," said Katie.

"What grade are you?" he tapped Katie's arm vigorously.

She pulled away from him.

"You mean what grade are we in?" asked Esther.

"Yeah, what grade are you?"

"We're in fifth grade," Katie said.

"Oh, yeah. I forgot. I'm fifth grade, too."

"No, you're not, Louis," said Katie, sighing impatiently.

Louis frowned. "What grade am I?"

"You're in a special grade, Louis," said Esther quickly. "Your grade doesn't have a number."

"Oh, yeah." He walked in silence for a minute.

"We might see Renee on our way to school," Esther said. "She lives somewhere near here."

"Who's Rrr-nay?" Louis asked.

"I hope so," said Katie, ignoring him. "I can't wait to meet her!"

Esther looked at her sideways. "Well, she's not that great. She's just another girl."

"None of us have been on TV," said Katie.

Esther shrugged. "None of us play the violin."

Just then the girls turned the corner onto Chestnut Street, and Katie noticed a tall, thin girl walking ahead of them. She had on a bright yellow dress with a blue bow in the back, and her hair was tied in one long, thick braid starting behind her left ear.

"Is that Renee?" Katie whispered excitedly.

Esther nodded. "You want to go meet her?"

"Yeah!"

"Me, too," said Louis. "I like girls."

Katie looked at Esther helplessly. "We can't take Louis with us," she whispered.

"Why not?"

"Well—we just can't. What would she think? She might think that—"

"That he's related to us?" questioned Esther.

"And we want her to like us, don't we?" said Katie. "We want her to feel at home here."

"But I think Louis should feel at home, too," Esther replied. "After all, he lives here."

"Never mind," said Katie. "We'll wait 'til we get to school."

The girls didn't say anything else. When they reached the school playground, Esther went to get Renee, and Katie took Louis over to the swing set.

"Why don't you swing, Louis?" said Katie. "You like to swing, don't you?"

Louis nodded vigorously.

"Okay, climb up into this swing, and I'll give you a push. Now hang on." Katie took the metal chains in her hands and pulled Louis and the swing back about a foot. He was so heavy that she couldn't pull him any further. Then she pushed him forward.

"Pump, Louis! Pump!" Katie shouted as she pushed.

"Higher!" Louis shouted. "Gimme a under-dog!"

Katie saw that Esther had found Renee. They were standing near the monkey bars. "I have to go talk to someone now," Katie told Louis. "You see how high you can get while I'm gone."

Katie walked over to the girls. "Hi," she said to Renee.

"Hi," said the new girl. Her eyes were small and narrow. Like Esther, she had a thin face, but she didn't have Esther's bright pixy glow.

"This is my friend, Katie," said Esther. "She lives across the street from me."

"I'm Renee St. Vincent," the girl told Katie. "I live on the other side of the block from you, but down a ways where all those new houses are being built. We live on the cul-de-sac called Cherry Court."

"Oh," said Katie, not knowing what else to say. She noticed that Renee was holding a brown case. "Is that your violin?" she asked.

Renee smiled at her. "Yes. My mother wants me to play for the music teacher today so I can be in the school orchestra. I've been playing since I was four."

"Wow," said Esther and Katie together.

"Our friend Jillian has been taking ballet lessons since she was three," said Esther.

"Who needs ballet lessons?" Renee answered. "Is she going to be a ballerina?"

Katie and Esther looked at each other but didn't say anything. Then Renee told them that she played classical music on her violin and had even auditioned for the All-State Children's Orchestra when she lived in Indiana.

"Were you really on TV?" Katie asked her.

"Yes. But that was when I was eight."

"What show were you on?" asked Esther, her blue eyes wide.

Renee lifted her chin slightly and said, "I was on a famous Indiana show. You don't get it here."

"That's too bad," said Katie. "I was hoping to see you on the reruns."

"Do you like Minnesota, Renee?" Esther asked seriously. She had always lived at 126 Maple Lane.

Renee shrugged. "It's all right. Mom says that Indiana isn't nearly as cold in the winter. And I don't think it ever gets this humid in the summer, either. Doesn't anyone around here have a pool?"

The girls shook their heads.

Renee continued, "Our neighbors in Indiana had a swimming pool with a diving board and a slide. We could swim every day in the summer if we wanted to."

"We go to the swimming hole when it's hot," said Katie, smoothing her straight, dark brown hair away from her face. "In fact, we're going today. Do you want to come?"

"No, thank you. I—I have to practice my violin."

Esther glanced at Renee's violin case again and said, "I hope Miss Lauren is still our music teacher."

"She is," said Renee. "The principal told my mother. She's the one I'm supposed to play my violin for."

Miss Lauren was the prettiest teacher in the whole school. Everyone loved her. She taught them funny songs and let them play flutophones and tambourines and Autoharps. She even played the guitar.

"Miss Lauren always has Jillian sing the solo parts in music class," Katie said.

"Yes, I know," said Renee. "Jillian and I have decided to be best friends."

"Jillian is Tracy's best friend," Katie said, feeling disappointed about Renee's choice.

Esther chewed her lip, looking thoughtful.

"Who's Tracy?" Renee asked as her eyes wandered over the playground.

"You know," said Esther. "She's the short, black-haired girl who sat next to Jillian during Sunday school."

"Oh, you mean the fat girl?"

"Y-yes," Esther said. Quickly she added, "Tracy is so nice. We all like her."

"Oh, yes," Renee said with a yawn. "She's the one who asked all those stupid questions during the Bible lesson."

"My mom says that not everyone can be the smartest," said Esther. "After all, Tracy is young for our class. Her birthday's not until the summer."

Renee gave a laugh. "So? I'm younger than all of you—I turned nine this month. I skipped a grade when I was little."

Just then Jillian and Tracy arrived. Jillian left Tracy by the curb and ran to Renee. Tracy followed slowly, her lips in a little red pout between her round cheeks.

"Hi, Jillian," said Renee.

"Hi, Renee," Jillian said, tossing her pretty red curls. "I was hoping you'd be here already. The playground can be so boring."

"I love the playground," said Renee.

"Oh—well—I like the playground too," Jillian stammered. "It's just that boys are so noisy—"

"Who's the one hanging from the monkey bars?" Renee asked.

A blond-haired boy was swinging upside down, yelling to his friends, while his T-shirt settled in his armpits.

"It's Barry Logan," Katie said.

"He's a showoff," said Renee, catching his eye and turning away.

The principal's voice came over the loudspeaker telling everyone to assemble in the school auditorium.

"That's just the cafeteria," Katie explained to Renee.

"I know what an auditorium is," Renee answered.

Katie looked down at the blacktop. She wondered if Renee knew about everything.

"Come on, Renee," said Jillian. "I'll show you where to go, if you want."

The girls began walking toward the square brick building.

"Ka-tie! Es-ther!" A loud, slurred voice rang out over the playground.

Louis left the swing set and ran toward the girls. His jeans were covered with dust and sand, and the hem of his shirt was hanging over his belt. His thick tongue hung out of his mouth while he panted.

"I swinged high," he said to Katie.

"Good for you," she said, flushing.

"Good for me!" He laughed loudly.

Suddenly Barry shouted from the monkey bars. "Hey, retard! How're you doin'?"

"What're you doin' in school, retard?" hollered Joel Kirby, who was climbing up the bars.

Katie glared at him. Joel was always making fun of Louis. "You're not much smarter, Joel, so you better be quiet!" she yelled back.

"Well, if it isn't Miss 'A' Student!" he said.

"You leave her and Louis alone!" said Esther. "Don't listen to them, Louis. They're stupid."

"Yeah, stupid," he said. He turned and looked at Jillian and Renee. "What's their name?"

"That's Jill, Louis. You know her," Katie said, walking quickly, trying to hurry the girls into the school building.

"And this is Renee," said Esther, stopping to make introductions.

"Rrr-nay," he smiled. "Hi, Rrrnay. I'm Louis. I'm twelve."

Renee had been watching Louis and the others through narrow eyes. Katie thought that Renee looked like a scared stray cat, hiding in a dark corner, hungry.

When Louis spoke to Renee, she flushed. The color started at her ears and crept over her whole face.

"Let's go inside, Jillian," she said, turning away from him. "We're going to be late."

Chapter Two

The New Girl

Mrs. Tuttle had short brown hair, and her long, skinny legs stretched from her hemline to her brown loafers. From behind brown-rimmed glasses, she beamed at Katie and the other students in her classroom.

"Now everybody find your desks. You're seated alphabetically. I've put name tags on your desks, so I'll get to know you in no time. Hurry, hurry. We have lots to do today. Everyone quiet."

Katie's desk was in the first row by the window. On the front of the desk, her name was written on yellow paper in perfect cursive writing. She waved at Esther, who sat on the other side of the room. Katie noticed that Renee sat toward the back, and Tracy Sumner got to sit right next to her. Tracy was fidgeting with her book bag. Katie wished she could trade places with Tracy and sit by Renee.

Katie looked out the window at the playground and the rows of swings lined up in front of the steel fence. The sunlight reflected off the slides and made them look like silver.

She wondered what Renee would want to do during recess. Esther had brought her jump rope. Sometimes the girls jumped rope; sometimes they played four square with a big rubber ball.

Before long, Katie and her friends were eating their sack lunches in the cafeteria. Renee got to buy her lunch. She came back to the table with pizza and canned fruit on her tray and sat down next to Jillian. The girls all looked at the pizza longingly.

"Do you guys always bring lunches?" Renee asked them.

"Yeah. My mom says it's more economical," said Katie.

"Oh." Renee picked up her piece of pizza and let the cheese stretch as she bit into it.

"I think it'd be nice to buy lunch," said Jillian as she eyed the pizza.

Katie thought so too, but she sat quietly and ate her bologna sandwich. Her mom had given her a chocolate pudding cup, and she ate that next.

"Is that pudding?" Renee asked. "If I ever bring a lunch, I'm going to have my mother put one of those in it."

Katie smiled and wiped her mouth. "I like it too."

"What's that on your napkin?" Renee peered across the lunch table.

Katie blushed slightly. "It's writing. Sometimes my mom writes me a note on my napkin."

Everyone looked to Renee for her reaction. Katie felt a nervous tug inside. She hoped Renee wouldn't laugh.

"What does it say?" she asked.

"It says, 'Have a good first day. I love you, Mom'."

Renee glanced away.

Katie let out a breath.

At recess they all played four square. The winner from the day before always got to start off in the fourth square, but since it was the first day of school the girls let Renee start there. Then Katie almost wished they hadn't let her, because no one could get her out.

All day Katie had been looking forward to music class with Miss Lauren. When Mrs. Tuttle called the students to line up at the classroom door, Katie hurried to join them.

But Renee was the first person in line, and she was carrying her violin.

"What's that?" hissed Joel Kirby, pointing to Renee's case.

"It's a violin, stupid," said Jillian.

"Why does she have it?"

Jillian laughed at him. "Because she's going to play it, what do ya think?"

The other children giggled, and Mrs. Tuttle said, "Shh!"

Miss Lauren stood at her door, smiling at all the children as they came into the room. When everyone was seated, she went to the front of the class and smiled at them again. She had wispy gold hair that rippled down her back and large, blue-green eyes the color of clear lake water. And she had very long, brown eyelashes.

"It's nice to have you in class today," she said in a voice that sounded like music. "Let's get acquainted and sing some songs. Some of you I don't even know. Let's start in front and tell everyone our names."

"I'm Renee St. Vincent, I'm from Indiana, and I've played the violin for six years," Renee said.

Miss Lauren smiled at her. "My goodness! I guess you're the new girl who will be in my orchestra."

"Yes, Ma'am. Would you like me to play for you?"

"Certainly. But we'll wait until the end of class."

Renee sighed and looked out the window while Katie and the rest of the children gave their names. Miss Lauren took several minutes talking about the new songs they would sing and the instruments they would learn to play. Then Miss Lauren played her guitar while the class sang.

After the singing Miss Lauren said happily, "We will also have a Thanksgiving program that you will be in. There will be singing parts and speaking parts and even instrumental parts."

"Will the orchestra play?" asked Renee.

"Yes, Renee, but wait until I call on you before you ask a question."

"Yes, Ma'am."

Miss Lauren gave a dimpled smile. "All right, class, I'm afraid it's time to leave."

Renee raised her hand.

"Yes, Renee?" said Miss Lauren.

"May I play for you before I go back?"

"Certainly. Everyone line up and keep quiet while Renee plays."

Katie watched closely as Renee took out her violin and bow. The violin was a shiny red-brown, with beautiful black curlicues carved into the top. Renee played a few awful-sounding notes and tightened the black knobs on the neck of the instrument.

She raised the violin to her chin, arched her hand and fingers, and drew the bow across the strings. The other children in line turned around to stare while she played. Katie's mouth dropped open. Miss Lauren smiled with pleasure.

Mrs. Tuttle came for the children, but no one left. When Renee finished playing, Miss Lauren and Mrs. Tuttle clapped.

"Beautiful, Renee, just beautiful!" exclaimed Miss Lauren. "Sonata Number Five by Bach, wasn't it?"

"Yes, Miss Lauren." Renee smiled at her.

"I hope she's not going to play every time we have music class," groaned Joel.

"Music class goes slow enough already," Barry said.

Katie thought gym class went slower than music class. In gym she always dropped the ball or threw it to the wrong person.

Mrs. Tuttle's class had gym on the soccer field today. The grass was no longer wet, and the sun beat down on the children as they listened to Mrs. Tuttle. Katie turned her face to catch the breeze.

Katie noticed the special education class out on the playground near the soccer field. Louis was swinging high on the swing set, singing loudly, his pink cheeks and little nose pointed to the sky. The swing's chains clanked as they straightened out on every downswing. Louis saw her and waved.

"Hi, Ka-tie!" he shouted.

Katie blushed as a few of her classmates looked at her and Louis. Renee didn't seem to hear.

"Today we're going to play dodge ball," Mrs. Tuttle was saying. "Remember, when you get hit by a ball, you must go to the trench on the other team's side. And remember—no hitting above the waist. Okay, let's pick teams. Joel, you can be the captain of one team. Barry, you're captain of the other team. Joel, you start choosing."

Joel and Barry began with their friends and worked their way down to the girls. Barry had first pick.

He looked steadily at Renee. "You," he mumbled.

"Who, Barry?" questioned Mrs. Tuttle. "Renee?"

"Yes."

Joel frowned. "Uh—then I guess I'll take Jillian."

And so the choosing ran on. Katie hoped that Barry would pick her so that she could be on Renee's team. Renee seemed like the type of girl who never lost a game. But Joel picked both Katie and Esther about halfway through the girls.

Pretty soon only Tracy and Corey Shark were left, and it was Barry's turn to choose. Katie wondered which one he would pick. Corey was about the dirtiest, scrawniest girl in the whole school. But Tracy always got out right away.

Barry and Renee studied the two remaining girls. Renee surveyed Tracy's round figure with a look of disgust.

"Pick the skinny one," she said to Barry. "She ought to be able to stay in awhile."

Tracy blushed.

Esther glared at Renee, but Katie looked at the ground. She felt sorry for Tracy.

The game began with the boys picking off opponents one at a time, while most of the girls hovered in the back until the trench began filling up and balls began flying from behind them. Katie, Esther, and the other girls skittered to the sides of the field, glancing back and forth between the center line and the trench line while the boys played.

Then Renee began to fight for a ball. After getting a few girls out along the sides, she began aiming for some of the boys. She had no success against them until Joel caught someone's ball and she caught a pop ball off the one he was holding in his hands.

"You're out!" she shouted at him across the line.

"Am not! It didn't hit me!"

"Did too! It hit your hand, and I caught it!"

On the sidelines, Mrs. Tuttle blew her whistle. "Joel—you're out. Go to the trench."

He threw his ball on the ground and made a face at Renee as he passed her. She smiled triumphantly, wound up, and threw a hard ball at Tracy, who was still standing near the sideline.

It smashed into Tracy's arm. A red flush started near her round shoulder and began spreading down to her elbow. Holding the sore spot with her other hand, Tracy headed toward the opposite trench. Katie could see that tears were filling her eyes. Esther ran over to Tracy and put an arm around her.

"It's okay, Tracy," she said. "Why don't we go over and stand by Mrs. Tuttle for the rest of the game?"

"My eyes are just watering—because—it stings," Tracy sniffed.

Another ball came whizzing over the line and slammed into both of the girls.

Mrs. Tuttle blew her whistle. "Barry—that's enough. What did you mean by hitting them like that? Tracy's already out."

"I didn't mean to hit her," he said.

"If you children don't stop being so rough, we're not going to play this again," said Mrs. Tuttle sternly. "Tracy, are you all right?"

She nodded, sniffing loudly.

"You and Esther come stand by me. Barry and Renee, you be more careful. Time's almost up. Finish out the game."

There weren't many kids left. Katie had managed to survive by staying away from flying balls. But she was soon put out by a fly ball from Renee that she tried to catch, but dropped.

"Sorry, Katie," called Renee, with a smile.

Katie smiled back.

"Wait for me after gym class," Renee said when Katie passed her to go to the trench. Katie grinned at her.

The game was soon over, with Renee and Barry the victors. The boys stood around Renee for a minute to tell her she was a good player.

"Sorry I had to get you out," Renee said as Katie passed the group of boys standing with Renee.

Katie stopped and shrugged her shoulders. "That's okay. You got a lot of other people out too."

"Yeah, I know. But I really like you."

"You do?" Katie said. "Thanks! I like you too."

Renee walked off the soccer field with Katie.

Katie kicked a few pebbles with her toe. "Renee—do you want to come over to my house and play tomorrow? I've got lots of doll stuff."

"Sure! That sounds fun," said Renee, smiling. "You can come over to my house, too. I think I'll even have a slumber party next week. That sounds wonderful, doesn't it?"

"Yeah! I love slumber parties," said Katie.

"It'll be fun! We'll have cake and ice cream and play games—"

"I can't wait!" said Katie, giggling.

"Ka-tie!" a loud voice called.

Renee stepped away from Katie as Louis bounded up to them. "He sure likes you, doesn't he?" she said scornfully, twisting the tails of her blue sash around her fingers.

"Yeah, I guess so. Louis is—he's my neighbor. His mom and my mom work together. They both teach the special education classes here. But my mom is a substitute teacher."

"We're buddies," said Louis, putting his arm around Katie's shoulder.

"Louis, don't do that," Katie said as she moved his arm.

"You play with me today?" Louis asked her.

Katie saw that Renee was watching them, backing up another step and growing pink. "I'm playing with Esther today, Louis," Katie said, beginning to walk away from him.

"Tomorrow," said Louis decidedly.

"If you're playing with him, you're not playing with me," Renee stated. And then she hurried off.

Chapter Three

Louis, the Actor

"Aren't we supposed to bring Louis home today?" Esther asked Katie that afternoon as they walked away from Jefferson Elementary toward Maple Lane.

Katie shrugged. "All we have to do is make sure he gets across the streets. And the only street where the patrols won't cross him is our street. We'll wait for him up here at the corner."

"Why didn't we just wait for him at school?" said Esther, looking at her.

Katie was avoiding the cracks in the sidewalk, taking giant steps where she could, and little steps when she couldn't reach for a big one. She stepped over a few more cracks before she answered quietly, "I thought Renee might want to walk home with us. She lives over on Cherry Court, you know."

Esther frowned slightly. "I'm glad she didn't," she said, "because I thought she was mean in gym class."

"Esther!"

"Well, she *was* mean. You would've thought so too, if she hadn't been so nice to you."

"It was only a game, Esther," said Katie, skipping another crack.

"But she hurt Tracy's arm. And she hurt Tracy's feelings too."

"Tracy's feelings are always getting hurt."

"That's because she thinks nobody likes her."

"We all like her," Katie said impatiently, "and she knows that."

"Renee doesn't like her," said Esther.

"Renee doesn't even know her yet."

"I don't think she'll like me either." Esther's blue eyes stared straight ahead, and Katie couldn't tell whether Esther wanted Renee to like her or not.

"Of course she'll like you, Esther. Everybody at school likes you."

"Ka-tie! Es-ther!" Louis shouted behind them.

The girls stopped and turned around. Louis was running down the sidewalk toward them. He was holding several papers in one hand and his big Snoopy lunch box in the other.

Katie thought Louis looked like an old man when he ran. His tongue hung from his mouth, and he watched his feet, as if consciously placing one in front of the other. His steps were heavy—like boots—pounding on the cement.

Louis began waving his papers and yelling, "I drawed these!"

But he lost his grip, and the breeze blew the papers out of his hand and across the sidewalk into people's front lawns. "My pictures!" wailed Louis.

"Oh, Louis," said Katie, disgusted.

"Don't cry, Louis," Esther consoled him. "We'll get them all back."

Katie and Esther ran about chasing the papers. Soon Louis had them in his hands. "Now if you drop them again, you're gonna pick them up," said Katie.

"Look," said Louis, smiling and holding out a paper covered with multicolored crayon marks.

"That's pretty," said Esther, patting his arm.

"What is it?" asked Katie.

"It's Ka-tie and Es-ther. My buddies." He grinned at them.

Esther smiled. "That's very nice, Louis."

Katie squinted at the paper. It looked like a bunch of scribbles to her. A mass of green and blue lines circled the paper, with yellow and pink blobs in the middle.

"You don't like it?" Louis asked, his blue eyes clouding with disappointment.

Katie looked at him. His round face was still flushed from running. His thick, grooved tongue rested on his bottom lip. The folds of skin beside his nose made his eyes seem far apart.

Then Katie read the look in those eyes. She glanced down at the picture, trying to hide the blush that began spreading over her cheeks. "Y-yes," she said quietly. "I think your picture is beautiful."

Louis grinned. "You take it. It's a pres-ent." He handed her the drawing.

"Thank you, Louis. I'll hang it up in my room."

Esther smiled. "Come on, let's go home now."

The three crossed the street together and walked down Maple Lane to Louis's house. The girls walked him to the gate.

"Good-bye, Louis," said Katie, glancing down the street at her white frame house with the porch that wrapped around two sides. "We've gotta go now."

"Come play," he begged.

"We can't," said Esther. "We're going to the swimming hole."

"Esther!" Katie exclaimed.

"I come too!" said Louis.

"Whoops." Esther sneaked a glance at Katie.

"No, Louis," said Katie. "We're not going to the swimming hole after all."

"Oh," he said sadly.

Katie opened the gate for him. "See ya later, Louis."

"Hello there, girls!" called Mrs. Williams from the front door. She and Katie's mom walked out onto the porch, so the girls went inside the yard with Louis.

Katie's mom was wearing a bib apron trimmed with eyelet lace. Her wavy brown hair was the same color as her daughter's. "How was your first day?" she asked, coming down the sidewalk and giving Katie a hug.

"I met a new girl today," Katie answered. "Her name is Renee St. Vincent, and she's really neat."

Esther looked at the ground and didn't say anything about Renee.

"Oh, that's nice," said Mrs. Crawford. "Where does she live?"

"On Cherry Court. They even go to our church."

"Well, good. I'll have to invite her mother over for tea one of these days." She brushed Katie's bangs out of her eyes. "What are you and Esther doing this afternoon?"

"I dunno," Katie said, glancing at Esther. "I guess we could put on a play or something." She thought over all the fairy tales and other stories that she and Esther had put on for their mothers. They always acted out all the parts, and sometimes they even dressed up in old clothes to look like the characters.

"My mom can't come," said Esther. "Luke's at home sick today."

"Well, we have to have an audience bigger than one person," said Katie.

"How about Louis?" suggested Mrs. Crawford.

Katie and Esther looked at each other, disappointed. Katie wished she were at home so that she could tell her mom she'd rather not have him over.

Mrs. Williams beamed at the girls. "Louis would love that! Louis, dear, you're going to get to watch Katie and Esther do a play for you!"

Louis clapped his hands and smiled.

"Which one should we do?" Esther asked Katie as Louis quietly walked over to his mom and tugged on her sleeve.

"Momma, what's—a play?" he whispered.

"A play is a story acted out," said Mrs. Williams. "Remember when you saw *The Wizard of Oz* on TV? It's like that."

"Oh, goody!" said Louis. "Are you gonna be the Wiz of Oz?"

"No," said Katie. "That's too long."

"Better do a fairy tale so Louis can understand," said Katie's mom.

"We used to do 'Rumplestiltskin' when we were little girls," said Esther.

"Rrrumplisk—Rrrumpska—what's that?" asked Louis trying to form the word.

"Rumplestiltskin," said Katie quickly. "Come on, if we're going to do this, let's get started." She turned to leave; Esther and Louis followed her.

"I'd better go supervise. Come over in about half an hour to see the performance, Eda," said Katie's mom to Mrs. Williams. "And thanks for telling me how the conference went with the school board today. Let me know when they reach a decision."

"I will! You can be sure of that. It'll be a tremendous answer to prayer," responded Louis's mother.

Katie wondered what her mother and Mrs. Williams were talking about, but she didn't ask any questions. She was too busy hoping that Louis wouldn't interfere with their play.

As soon as they all reached Katie's house, the girls pushed aside two armchairs in the living room so that they would have room for their stage. Then Katie assigned the places for entrances and exits and made Louis sit quietly on the sofa as the audience. Katie was to be the miller's daughter; Esther was to be the miller, the king, and Rumplestiltskin.

They had barely begun practicing when Louis said, "Where's Rrrumple—where's Rrrum-plastic—you know, where is he?"

"It's Rumplestiltskin," said Esther, laughing.

"He doesn't come in until the miller's daughter goes to the castle with the king. The miller has to brag that his daughter can spin straw into gold first," Katie said.

"What's straw?"

"It's hay," said Esther. "Like what a scarecrow wears."

"What's gold?"

"It's money," said Katie. "No more questions now. We have to get on with the story."

Esther brought in a blue chair they always used for their plays. As the miller's daughter, Katie was told to sit and spin straw into gold or she would die. She put her face in her hands and began to weep.

Louis jumped up and went over to pat her shoulder. "It's okay, Ka-tie. Don't cry."

Katie raised her head and glared at him. "Louis, I'm just pretending. Go sit down."

Louis returned to his seat, and Esther hopped into the scene and offered to spin the gold if Katie would give her the necklace she was wearing.

"Are you Rrrusk-la-skin?" Louis asked Esther.

She nodded and put a finger to her lips.

But Louis asked loudly, "Ka-tie, can I be Rrrumpla—Rrruskl-mat-skin?"

Just then Katie's mother came in from the kitchen. "How's it going?"

Katie heaved a sigh. "Louis keeps interrupting."

"He's probably bored sitting there while you two do everything. Maybe you could let him have a part."

"But he wants to be Rumplestiltskin!" said Esther.

"And he can't even say the name," Katie added.

"Oh, Katie," said her mother, "let Louis be Rumplestiltskin. He'll be cute."

"He's supposed to be a dwarf, Mom. Louis is bigger than Esther and me put together."

Mrs. Crawford gave her a warning look as she headed for the kitchen again. "It's only a play," she said.

"Oh, all right," said Katie. "Come here, Louis, so Esther can show you what to do."

After the instruction, Louis went off-stage to wait. Katie rested her head in her arms again.

Louis sneaked in behind her. "Rrroarrr!"

Katie screamed.

"Louis!" exclaimed Esther.

He laughed. "I got you, Ka-tie!"

"Louis, you're not a monster," said Esther. "You're a short little bearded man who comes to spin the gold. Don't act like a monster!"

"If you scare me again, you can't be Rumplestiltskin," Katie said severely. "And I haven't even cried yet. You have to give me some time to cry a little before you come in."

Louis went out again and left Katie to cry. Katie cried and cried and motioned for Louis to come in. Instead, Louis tiptoed through the dining room and kitchen and went into the front hall.

"Louis!" Katie moaned. "What are you doing?"

Louis peeked around the doorway and tiptoed back into the living room toward the blue chair. He put two fingers over his head and hit his mouth with the palm of his hand in an Indian war cry. Then he made his attack. Katie climbed up on the chair and screamed at him. "Louis! Stop it! Stop it! This is 'Rumplestiltskin,' not Cowboys and Indians! Can't you do anything right?"

Louis stopped, looking at her through wide eyes. Then he went to the sofa and buried his face in a pillow and began to sniffle.

"Louis, we're not done with the play yet," said Esther.

"I don't care," mumbled Louis.

"Well, if he's going to be like that, let's forget it," said Katie. "I don't want to do this, anyway."

"Louis, if you don't come back, I'm going to be Rumplestiltskin instead of you," said Esther.

Louis hopped off the sofa and returned to the stage.

The girls tried several times to teach Louis to say "Rumplestiltskin" so it would sound right when he had

to jump around his campfire and sing about his name. But he couldn't learn it.

"Let's skip the campfire part," said Katie. "I'll just guess his name right, and the play will be over."

Soon Mrs. Williams came to watch. She and Katie's mother told the girls that the play was a success. Katie was just glad it was over because then Mrs. Williams took Louis home with her. Katie wanted to forget that the whole afternoon had ever happened.

But at supper that night while they ate their spaghetti and meatballs, Mrs. Crawford announced to the family that Katie and Esther had done a play with Louis after school.

Katie's dad was seated across from Katie at the round oak table. His shoulders were so broad that Katie couldn't see any of the chair behind him. He raised his dark, bushy eyebrows and said to her, "You did? That was very thoughtful, Princess."

Katie shrugged. "It was just 'Rumplestiltskin.' And it wasn't very good."

The lines beside Mr. Crawford's eyes crinkled as he grinned at her. "I'm sure it was. Were you the princess or the prince?"

"Daddy, there isn't any prince or princess in 'Rumplestiltskin!' " Katie said, laughing. "There's a miller's daughter, and the king—"

He laughed. "Oh, yes, the miller's daughter—"

"Who was Louis?" asked Katie's thirteen-year-old brother, Jeffers. He sucked up his spaghetti noodles and licked the extra tomato sauce from his lips.

"Jeffrey, wrap the noodles around your fork. Don't eat like that," said Mrs. Crawford, handing him a napkin.

"Louis was Rumplestiltskin." Katie moaned after taking another bite. "He was awful."

"Katie, he was a cute Rumplestiltskin," said her mother. "You only did the play in front of Mrs. Williams and me, anyway. It didn't have to be perfect."

Katie shrugged.

"I thought Louis did very well for on-the-spot training," Mrs. Crawford continued. "You know, he's never been in a play before."

"There was a disabled kid at the junior high today," said Jeffers. "Everybody was making fun of him, and the teachers couldn't make him understand what rooms he was in or anything. I felt kinda bad for him."

"That's a shame," said Mrs. Crawford. "I wonder why he's not in our special education class at Jefferson. Maybe he's too old."

"I don't know how you do it," said Jeffers, shaking his head.

Mr. and Mrs. Crawford exchanged glances.

"Do what?" asked Mrs. Crawford slowly.

"Work with the disabled kids at school."

Mrs. Crawford gave him a long look before she answered. "I enjoy working with them. They're children who can learn—children with feelings just like anybody else—but they need special attention."

"You know, either of you could have been born disabled," said Mr. Crawford. "It's not necessarily inherited. It just happens."

Jeffers' mouth dropped open. "I'm sure glad I wasn't!"

"Me either," said Katie. "I wouldn't want to be Louis for anything."

Mr. Crawford's brown eyes looked steadily into Katie's, and she squirmed. Whenever he looked at her like that, she felt as though he could read her mind.

"I think it would be good for you kids to put yourselves in Louis's place once in a while," he said.

He looked down to finish his meal. The others ate without saying much. Then Mr. Crawford smiled at his quiet children.

"I'm proud of you kids, you know that," he said. "I only want you to learn whenever you can. Now why don't we have our devotions and see what the Lord has for us tonight."

He got his Bible from a nearby counter top and sat back down at the table. He turned the thin pages with his broad hands that were stained with varnish. "Okay, where are we tonight? Let's see: Matthew, chapter 18, verses 1 through 6."

Mr. Crawford began to read:

> At the same time came the disciples unto Jesus, saying, Who is the greatest in the kingdom of heaven?
>
> And Jesus called a little child unto him, and set him in the midst of them,
>
> And said, Verily, I say unto you, Except ye be converted, and become as little children, ye shall not enter into the kingdom of heaven.
>
> Whosoever therefore shall humble himself as this little child, the same is greatest in the kingdom of heaven.
>
> And whoso shall receive one such little child in my name receiveth me.
>
> But whoso shall offend one of these little ones which believe in me, it were better for him that a millstone were hanged about his neck, and that he were drowned in the depth of the sea.

"What do you think this passage of Scripture is saying?" Mr. Crawford asked his children.

Neither spoke. Katie wondered why the Bible sometimes said things that made her heart feel like it was being pricked with a pin.

"There is a great lesson here that I want you both to learn," Mr. Crawford said. "Your mother and I need to remember it too. None of us is greater than anyone else. No Christian is more important than another Christian, but we often think we are."

Katie looked down at the table, listening hard.

After a pause, Mr. Crawford went on, "Adults think they're more important to God than children. And many times children think they're more important than other children, maybe because they're smarter or more talented. But it's not true. Jesus told the disciples that they must become humble like a small child who has to rely on God for everything."

Now Katie wished she hadn't screamed at Louis during the play practice.

"Jeffers, what does verse 5 mean?" Mr. Crawford passed his Bible to his son.

Jeffers read it slowly. " 'And whoso shall receive one such little child in my name receiveth me.' Does it mean that the way we treat others is the way we treat God?"

"Yes, I think so. Very good. Princess, read verse 6, and tell me what you think."

Katie took his Bible and read the last verse. " 'But whoso shall offend one of these little ones which believe in me, it were better for him that a millstone were hanged about his neck, and that he were drowned in the depth of the sea.' "

Katie looked up at her father. His eyes were fixed on her face. "Well?" he said.

She nodded. "It sounds scary."

"God is warning us here to curb our pride," he answered. "This verse is only scary to those who disobey God."

Chapter Four

Saturday Discoveries

Katie was dusting the living room Saturday morning when the phone rang.

"Hello?" said her mother's voice from the kitchen. ". . . Just a minute, please. Katie! Telephone!"

"Who is it?" Katie asked.

"I don't know. It's not Esther."

Katie ran into the kitchen and picked up the receiver. "Hello? . . . Oh, hi, Renee! How are you? . . . I'm not doing anything this afternoon. . . . Yeah, I'd love to. . . . One? Yeah, that's fine. . . . Uh, no, you don't need to come to my house. Where's yours again? . . . Can you just meet me halfway? . . . Okay, I'll bring some of my doll stuff. . . . See ya later! 'Bye."

Katie hung up the phone, smiling to herself. Mrs. Crawford took a batch of chocolate chip cookies out of the oven. "You're going to Renee's house this afternoon?"

"Is that okay? I forgot to ask you."

"Is it okay with her mother?"

"Yes. Does that mean I can go?" Katie asked.

Her mother put a new pan of cookies in the oven and set the timer. "Sure, you can go. Is anyone else playing with you?"

Katie paused. "Uh—I don't think so."

"You don't think so?"

"Renee didn't say anything about anybody else."

"Then if Esther's not playing too, you'd better give her a ring so she knows not to come over. You know you always play together on Saturday."

Katie fidgeted nervously with her dust rag. "Do I have to call her?" she asked. "We never really said anything about today."

"What about today?" said Mr. Crawford as he opened the kitchen door. He had been working out in his shop and had on his long blue apron splattered with stain and paint. He went to the sink and scrubbed his brown hands under hot running water.

"About Katie playing with Esther today," said Mrs. Crawford.

"Oh," he said.

Mrs. Crawford took the cookies off the cookie sheet and put them on the cooling rack.

"Are they ready to eat yet?" Mr. Crawford asked.

"No, let them cool for a minute, dear," said Mrs. Crawford. Then she turned to her daughter. "Yes, you need to call and tell Esther. How's she supposed to know you're going to Renee's house?"

Katie looked away. She wondered how she would tell Esther that she couldn't play today. She wondered if Esther would be mad.

While Katie and her mother were talking, Mr. Crawford stuck two fingers into the mixing bowl and put a glob of cookie dough into his mouth.

"Alan, you're as bad as the kids," said Mrs. Crawford.

"I can't help it that I married a good cook."

Mrs. Crawford laughed, and Katie went back into the living room.

Her dad's voice drifted in from the kitchen. "I like the way Katie's making new friends."

"So do I," Mrs. Crawford answered. "I was a little worried the other day that she was beginning to get snobbish. You know, about Louis and all."

"I guess there's always a problem with kids who have mental disabilities," said Mr. Crawford.

"If Katie were around Louis more, she would realize that he's a person just like she is," said Mrs. Crawford. "Perhaps she can come to the new Center for the disabled when it opens up. Eda Williams hasn't heard the final decision from the school board about that yet."

"Would you be working there all day?" he asked.

"Most likely. There aren't many adults willing to work with the disabled children. I probably wouldn't be home until five or so. At least you'd be here when the kids got home from school. I'd hate for them to come home to an empty house."

"Don't worry; it'll all work out," said Mr. Crawford.

By lunch time, Katie had finished her chores and had picked out some things to take to Renee's house. She had packed all her dolls, with one change of clothes for each, the bicycle, the car, and the dogs. She was still deciding whether she should take along any beds when she heard a light knock on her door.

"Yes?" she turned to see Esther in the doorway. Esther looked at Katie with inquisitive blue eyes.

"What are you doing?" she asked.

"Uh—playing—" Katie's face felt warm.

"Oh." Esther came in and climbed onto the brass bed and sat Indian-style. "I thought maybe we could go swimming today since we didn't go on Thursday."

"Mom says it's not going to be very hot today."

"Oh. Then how 'bout a play? Or a bike ride? That'd be fun!" Esther's eyes lit up with excitement.

"Yeah, I know, but—well, I can't play today." Katie pretended to hunt for something among her doll things.

"Why not?"

" 'Cause I'm going over to Renee's to play, that's all. I'm going right after lunch."

Esther's brows pulled together above her pug nose. "Oh." It was almost a whisper.

"But we can go for a bike ride on Monday if you want," Katie said hurriedly. "What do you want to do on Monday?"

Esther sat very quietly for a moment. Then she slid off the bed. "I don't care."

"Well, let's decide," said Katie.

"You decide," said Esther sharply. She left the room and went soundlessly down the stairs.

Katie got up and walked across the hall to her brother's room so that she could stand at the window overlooking the street.

The oaks and red maples lining the boulevard stretched their branches from the Crawfords' long windows to the middle of Maple Lane, and the trees on the Greshams' side of the street reached out to meet them.

Below, Esther walked out to the curb and glanced up the hill for traffic. A breeze rustled the leaves over her head, brushing her thin blond hair away from her face. The maple leaves were so thick that Katie lost sight of Esther as she crossed the street. But soon Esther's small figure emerged below the leaves, only to disappear into the big maroon house on the other side.

Katie gave a deep sigh.

"Hey, what are you doin' in my room?" said Jeffers from the hallway.

She turned reluctantly away from the window. "Nothin'."

He flopped across his bed and looked at her. "Then what's your problem?"

"Nothin'," she said again.

"Did you have a fight with Esther?"

"Never mind." She thrust her lip out and left the room.

All along the stairway were pictures of Katie and Jeffers when they had been little, and even old pictures of their parents. Katie paused and studied them as she headed downstairs. In her baby picture she had brown eyes that seemed very large for her small round face, and her head was practically bald, with only a little pink bow stuck on the top.

Katie's and Jeffers' school pictures from last year were hung on the wall, and so was Mr. and Mrs. Crawford's wedding picture. There was also a big picture of Katie and Jeffers lighting firecrackers at the park with all the Gresham kids. Katie looked at herself and Esther standing with their arms around each other's shoulders. Katie's brown head was tilted against Esther's blond one, and they were laughing as they smiled at the camera.

Katie sighed again and looked down the stairs at the front door, which faced the Greshams' house.

"Esther looked sad on her way out," Katie heard her mother say in the kitchen. "All she said was 'Good-bye, Mrs. Crawford'—real solemnly. It made me wonder exactly what Katie had said to her."

"I'm sure she was nice. It's not the end of the world if they don't play together one day," said Mr. Crawford.

Katie hesitated, and then she sat down on the step to listen.

"I know," said Mrs. Crawford. "I am a little concerned about Renee, though. I'm not sure I want Katie being with her too much. She was over here yesterday with Katie and Esther, and she seemed rather bossy—always had the last word on everything. She seems to intimidate them."

"She's probably a little nervous in her new surroundings. Like a fish out of water. She'll get over it soon, don't you think?"

Katie's muscles began to twitch. She moved down a step.

"Maybe," said Mrs. Crawford.

Mr. Crawford continued, "Katie brought Renee out to the shop yesterday. That girl acts like a miniature adult—she asked all kinds of intelligent questions."

"She's very tall, isn't she? Her mother says that Renee's height has been an advantage for her because it makes her look older than she is. She skipped a grade, you know. Her mother says she can compete better at that level."

"Hmm," said Mr. Crawford. "Isn't she a little young to be worried about competition? She's just a kid."

"At least she should be," said Mrs. Crawford quietly.

Katie's heart beat faster, and she tiptoed back upstairs until lunch was ready. Then as soon as lunch was over, she grabbed her bag of doll things.

"Good-bye, dear," said Mrs. Crawford, opening the back door for her. "Be polite while you're over there. And tell Mrs. St. Vincent I said hello."

"I will." Katie closed the door behind her and walked around the porch to the front.

The Greshams' house stood like a tall sentry across the street, the pointed black roof line standing at attention as it jutted into the sky. White drainpipes neatly edged the corners of the house, and black shutters trimmed the windows. Katie wondered if Esther were at a window, watching her. She shuffled up the sidewalk as quickly as she could without looking as though she were trying to escape.

Louis was swinging vigorously on the swing set in his yard.

"Ka-tie! Hi, Ka-tie!"

"Hi, Louis. Are you having fun today?"

He nodded, smiling. "We gonna play Rrrumpla-stlitz—Rrrumpla-stilt-skin today?"

"When did you learn how to say that?" Katie asked, stopping by the gate.

"Momma taught me how." Louis pumped his swing higher and grinned. "I like plays."

"Better slow down a little," said Katie. "You're going to break that swing set."

"No, I won't," he said.

Just then Mrs. Williams came out of her house. "Hi, Katie. Have you come over to play with Louis today? He sure enjoyed that play the other day. He hasn't stopped talking about it. He's done it several times for me already."

"All by himself?"

"Yes, he does all the parts. Quite a bit of running around that way, but he enjoys it." Mrs. Williams chuckled. "So, would you like to come in?"

"No, thank you. I'm on my way to Renee St. Vincent's house. She's the new girl in our class."

"Oh, my, isn't that nice. Esther's not going with you?"

"No, not today." Katie blushed a little.

"Oh, then maybe she would like to come play with Louis."

"Yes, maybe."

"I get a new school," said Louis.

"What new school?" asked Katie.

"My school," he said.

"Louis," said Mrs. Williams. "You're not supposed to talk about that, remember?"

"Oh, yeah. I forgot."

"What new school?" asked Katie, curious now.

Louis began giggling and putting his hand over his mouth. "I know, I know."

"Oh, I guess I can tell you, Katie. I was going to run over and tell the news to your mom today, anyway. I'm sure the school board will ask her to work there. The city's finally going to open a new training Center for the disabled."

"I thought they needed to build a building."

"They did. But the hardware store on Birch Street went out of business. The school board is going to buy and remodel it. We're going to have the Center open in less than two months!"

Chapter Five

The Closed Room

"Mom, this is Katie Crawford. Katie, this is my mother," said Renee when Katie stepped into the St. Vincents' new two-story house at 15 Cherry Court.

When Katie had walked up to Renee's house, she had thought it was the most beautiful house she'd ever seen. Outside there were flower boxes and bay windows. And there was even a room over the garage. Katie hoped that it was Renee's room so that she could see it. She always thought it would be nice to have a room set off from the rest of the house where she could sit and dream and play.

But inside, the house didn't feel quite like hers or Esther's. Katie could see her reflection in the parquet flooring in the front hall. The couch and chairs in the living room had curved wooden legs, and the cushions looked as though they had never been sat on.

"So this is Katie," said Mrs. St. Vincent with a smile. She looked like a queen, tall and elegant. Her soft gray hair was mixed with blond, and there were lines around her eyes and mouth. Katie thought she looked almost as old as Mrs. Williams, but Mrs. St. Vincent was pretty.

"I've heard a lot about you, Katie," she said. "All good, I promise. I'm glad you've made Renee feel at home here. Sometimes it's hard for Renee to make friends."

"Come on, Katie," said Renee. "Let's go play."

Katie looked at the stairway wall as they walked upstairs. It was wallpapered, with glossy wood banisters on both sides of the steps. "Hey, Renee," she said. "Don't you have family pictures of when you were little? I love looking at people's family pictures. Sometimes I make up stories about the people in the pictures—what they were like and what they were doing."

Renee answered, "We don't look at pictures, and we don't show them to other people."

Katie stared at Renee. She had never heard of a family without pictures. She and Esther loved to sit and look through their family photo albums.

There were several rooms along the upstairs hallway. Renee informed Katie that she and her older sister Amy had their own bedrooms. Then she said, "Jillian told me that Esther and her twin sisters have to share one room. I think that's horrible."

Katie was surprised by the statement. "I don't think they mind."

"My room's right here," said Renee. "There's a bunch of other rooms down there. Come on, let's play."

Katie was disappointed that Renee didn't live in the attic room. She glanced down the hall and noticed one closed door at the end. It must be the door to the attic room. All the other doors on the hallway were open.

"What is the attic room used for?" asked Katie.

"What attic?" said Renee, sitting down and emptying Katie's doll things on the floor.

"From outside it looks like there's a room above the garage. Is it someone's room?"

Two spots of pink showed on Renee's cheeks. She busied herself with the dolls and didn't answer.

"Is it Amy's room?" Katie asked, trying not to sound nosy.

"No. It's no one's room," Renee snapped. "Now are we going to play or talk about a stupid room?"

They set up all the things. Renee had a three-room doll house that they could use, but it wasn't really big enough for all the dolls. For her birthday in November Katie wanted the big town house that she had seen in the toy store at the mall. It was much nicer than Renee's doll house.

Renee divided up the dolls between them, giving Katie the dad and the smaller dolls who were the children. She kept the mother and teen-age daughter for herself.

"Let's play that the children just came home from school with their report cards, okay?" Renee said.

"Okay." Katie brought her dolls through the front door, calling, " 'Mom, we're home!' "

" 'Let me see your report cards, children. . . . My, you did very well. We'll have to give you a bonus on your allowance this week for every "A" you got. . . . What? What's this?' "

The mother looked at a different child's report card.

" 'You got a "C" in math? Why math ought to be your best subject!' " said Renee in a motherly voice.

" 'But I did my best,' " said Katie's doll.

" 'Well, I guess you're going to have to do better because a "C" is not good enough.' "

"You can't say that," said Katie, setting down her doll.

"Of course I can," said Renee. "She can't get a 'C.' That's terrible! That would make her about as stupid as Tracy." Renee laughed to herself.

Katie frowned. "But Tracy's parents are happy when she gets a 'C.' "

"Then it's no wonder that she doesn't get better grades. My mom would be mad if I got a 'C.' And I'd be embarrassed to get a 'B' or a 'C' on anything."

"Have your doll say something good about the report card," said Katie. "The mother's going to hurt her child's feelings."

"But all the grades are bad," said Renee matter-of-factly. " 'Now,' " she continued in the mother's voice, " 'we will have to see some improvement here. Look at your brother's and sister's report cards. They got good grades. So can you. You just need to work harder. No TV and no friends over until your grades come up.' "

"That's mean!" cried Katie.

"But she doesn't have any good grades."

"Yes, she does. She got an 'A' in art," Katie protested.

"Who cares about art?"

"I do. I love art."

"I hate it," said Renee.

"Can't you draw?" asked Katie.

"Of course I can draw. I just don't like it, that's all."

"You will like it when you meet Miss Carmichael. She's the best art teacher in the whole world."

"Is she the same Miss Carmichael that teaches your Sunday school class?" Renee asked.

"Yeah! Aren't her chalk drawings wonderful?"

Renee shrugged. "They're all right. I just don't like her—she's not very friendly."

"She is too!" exclaimed Katie. "She's even friendlier than Miss Lauren."

"No, she's not. I told Miss Carmichael that I would play my violin in Sunday school if she wanted me to, and she said that you usually don't have special music in Sunday school. I think it's terrible that we'll have to see her all the time—at church and school! I wish we didn't have to go to art. My sister says that art is an elective in high school. That means you don't have to take it."

"But we do all kinds of fun things in art!" said Katie, shocked. "We even have art contests before parent-teacher conferences, and the best picture from every grade goes on the bulletin board in the hallway."

"That's ridiculous. No one can tell which picture is the best."

"Miss Carmichael can."

"Who says she's right?"

"Well, it really doesn't matter. The rest of the pictures get hung up in the room, anyway."

"Do they get judged too?" Renee asked sharply.

"No. But at Jillian's slumber party last year, we all played a game where we had to draw a picture of someone in our class and the others had to guess who it was. It was a lot of fun. You would have liked it."

"No, I wouldn't."

Katie looked at Renee closely. Renee had a frown on her face, and she looked frustrated. Katie asked suddenly, "Do you only like to do the things you're good at?"

Renee seemed surprised; then she looked embarrassed. "Everyone likes to do things they're good at."

"Yeah," Katie said. "But I like to try other things too, even if I'm not good at them."

"So do I," said Renee, defensively.

"But you always seem to be better than everyone else. Like at grades, and four square, and dodge ball. How come you're like that?" Katie wondered what it would be like to be better at something than everyone else was.

"I—I have to be," she said. "It's the best way to be. Didn't your parents ever tell you that?"

"No. They say I should do as well as I can at everything. It doesn't really matter whether I get the best grades as long as I try, and it doesn't matter whether I win all the games I play."

Renee sat silently. Her face was solemn, and her eyes stared at the floor.

"Hey," said Katie, suddenly remembering, "when are we going to play all those games at your slumber party? When are you going to have it?"

Renee's ears began to turn red. "I don't know."

"You said it would be soon."

"Uh—Mother said that I can't have one now because—because—she doesn't think anyone's parents will want them to come over until they know us better."

"That's not true. My parents wouldn't mind at all if I came."

Renee's whole face was turning red. "No—that's okay. My—my grandmother is coming to visit us from Indiana, and—well, I—I just don't want to have everyone over yet, that's all. I'm going downstairs now to get us a snack. Stay right here."

Katie sat for a moment, thinking how strange it had been to see Renee frustrated like that. She wondered why Renee acted that way.

Katie got up to use the bathroom. She looked for it in all the open rooms on the hallway, and finally found it at the end of the hall, near the closed door. Katie couldn't help thinking about that attic room behind the door.

If she ever had an attic room, she would have it wallpapered in white, dotted with little pink rosebuds. There would even be wallpaper on the ceiling. Sheer, white curtains would flutter prettily every time she opened the windows. And on one whole side of the room, she would set up a giant doll house. Whenever Renee or the other girls came over, they would say that she had the most beautiful room they'd ever seen, and they would all want to come play with her and her doll things every day.

Katie looked at the closed door again. She wanted to peek. She glanced toward the stairway and listened for Renee's footsteps. Then she quickly reached for the doorknob.

The whole room was painted blue, even the walls that slanted upward to form the ceiling. The alphabet in block letters, with a picture for each letter, ran across one wall. The bedspread was covered with soldiers and drums. And at the foot of the bed, a toy box overflowed with balls of all sizes.

On one wall a painted bookcase held alphabet games, children's storybooks, and records. There were boxes of construction toys on the bottom shelves. A small indoor basketball hoop was stuck low on the wall.

Aa

Katie's heart pounded as she closed the door and slipped into the bathroom. She felt a little guilty and confused. And she wondered whose room it was.

Chapter Six

The Spelling Bee

"It's nippy out there," announced Mr. Crawford one morning as he entered the kitchen from the back porch. "I think winter's going to be early this year."

Mrs. Crawford sighed. "I wish the leaves didn't change color so fast. At this rate, we'll have snow before Thanksgiving."

"Oh, I hope so! I like having snow for my birthday," said Katie.

Mr. Crawford pulled out a kitchen chair and sat down. "Well, Princess, we'll just have to get out the almanac and read the weather prediction. I'd like to know how much snow we're in for this year, too."

"I don't want snow until football season is over," Jeffers said. "Last year we froze to death."

"I think that's enough blizzardy talk. I'm getting cold just thinking about it," said Mrs. Crawford as she put another heaping platter of pancakes on the table and sat down next to her husband. "Alan, there's a container of soup and some sandwich meat in the refrigerator. Think you can handle lunch by yourself today?"

"Why can't you come home?"

"We stay and eat with the children," she said, reaching over and squeezing his hand. "You can fend for yourself today, can't you?"

Mrs. Crawford laughed. "I guess I'm old enough for that."

"Is today the first day of your new job?" Jeffers asked.

"Yes it is, and I'm so excited!" said Mrs. Crawford. "They're planning on about thirty today."

"Wow," said Jeffers. "I didn't know there were that many mentally disabled people in Crescent City."

"They're not all mentally disabled, Jeffers," said Mr. Crawford. "Some of them are disabled physically because of an accident or because they were born that way."

"What do they do at the Center?" asked Katie.

"Well," said her mother, "the children with severe needs go to special classes to learn. Then we do crafts and play with them. The more independent adults will be taught a trade or hobby that will help them support themselves."

"Can disabled people live on their own?" Katie asked.

"Some can. It depends on how seriously disabled they are."

"Will Louis be at the Center?" asked Jeffers. "Do you think he'll be able to learn a trade?"

Mrs. Crawford sighed. "I don't know, dear. His mind is very simple."

"Yes, I know," said Katie. "He about drove us nuts when we did 'Rumplestiltskin' with him."

"Katie, he doesn't realize that he irritates people," said Mrs. Crawford.

Katie looked down at her plate.

"I kinda feel sorry for Louis when I see him," said Jeffers, "because he can't play sports or do normal things that other guys can do. I would be lonely if I never played with other guys."

"He is lonely," said Mr. Crawford. "Disabled people have feelings just like everyone else."

"We stick up for him when the kids at school call him names," said Katie eagerly, tossing her head.

Her parents exchanged glances.

"And why do you do that?" Mrs. Crawford asked slowly.

"Because the other kids need to see people being nice to him," she said.

"Katie," said her father, looking directly into her eyes with his deep brown ones. "You be kind to Louis because it is right, not because other kids are watching. You and your brother need to realize that God made Louis just the way he is, so there's nothing to feel sorry about. Louis is no worse off than you are, and you're no better than he is. God made him disabled for a reason, and God loves him in a very special way. Do you both understand that?"

Katie gulped and nodded. Jeffers was quietly studying the top of his pancake.

There was a silence while they ate their pancakes.

Then Mrs. Crawford asked Katie, "Did you say your class spelling bee is today, honey?"

She nodded.

"Don't need to worry about it," said Mr. Crawford. "You'll do fine." He got up from his chair and kissed her on the head.

"But I want to win again this year," said Katie. "Isn't that the best way to be?"

"No," said Mr. Crawford. "We just want you to try your hardest."

"Katie, I won't be here when you get home today, but Daddy'll be out in the shop. You'd also better take your warm coat this morning," said Mrs. Crawford.

"Won't my jacket be good enough?"

"I don't think so," said her dad, pulling on his work coat to go out to his shop. "It's windy today."

Mrs. Crawford looked out the window. "Sure is. And the temperature's only thirty. If it weren't so windy, there'd be a frost on the ground. Katie, are you walking to school with Esther this morning?"

Katie pushed back her plate and got up from the table. "I don't know."

"Well, you'd better hurry and get your coat. She and Luke are walking up the street already. I'll go tell them you're on your way."

"No—"

Katie's family looked at her.

She flushed a little. "We're not walking together today. Renee—Renee is coming to pick me up."

Mrs. Crawford looked at her husband.

"Renee acts like a big know-it-all," said Jeffers.

"She does know a lot," Katie said defensively. "And she's good at almost everything."

"Yeah, I know. She says that about every other sentence."

"You don't even know her," said Katie.

"Do too." Jeffers squinted at her from across the table. "You know what? You're starting to act just like Renee. You think you're too good for—"

"That's enough," said Mr. Crawford firmly. "Katie, run get your coat and leave for school before you're late. And Jeff, you learn to keep unkind opinions to yourself."

There was a knock at the back door, and Mrs. Crawford opened it. "Hello, Renee. Come on in."

"Hi, Mrs. Crawford. Hi, Katie. Are you ready to go?" Renee stepped inside and rubbed her mittened hands together. She had on rabbit-fur earmuffs and a ski jacket with the collar turned up around her throat. Her thick brown braid curled down over her shoulder.

"I've just got to get my coat," said Katie.

Katie soon forgot about the argument at breakfast. Today was the annual class spelling bee, and she loved it. To be put on the spot in front of all the other kids was a little frightening, but that's what made it so exciting. Katie thought it felt almost like being in a play, except that she couldn't memorize her part ahead of time. The most delicious feeling came over her whenever she spelled a word right.

"I hope I win the spelling bee today," said Renee on the way to school.

Surprised, Katie turned to look at her. "But I want to win it."

"So do I. I am glad I got to study vocabulary with you yesterday, Katie. I think one of us should win it."

"I won the spelling bee last year," said Katie.

"I won it every year in Indiana. Last year, I won the school spelling bee. I even beat all the sixth graders. If you ask me, I don't think this spelling bee is going to be very hard. The words she gave us for practice weren't difficult."

Katie stared at the sidewalk. Maybe spelling bee day wasn't going to be so great after all.

On the playground Jillian was excited about the spelling bee, but Tracy was dreading it.

"I'm going to get out on my first word; I know I will!" Tracy wailed. "It will be so embarrassing, and everyone will laugh at me."

No one denied it. Tracy always got out on her first word.

Katie had been watching Esther, who was standing with Luke and some of the sixth graders near the front doors. Esther looked small and fragile as she stood there, with the wind whipping across her skirt and blowing her hair in her face. Katie felt a lonely pain around her heart.

"It looks like Esther thinks she's too good for us now," Renee said. "Gotta talk with the older kids."

"She's just standing there," said Tracy.

"Of course she's standing," said Renee with a sneer. "We're all standing."

Katie fidgeted with her book bag. She wished they would stop talking about Esther like that. She hadn't done anything wrong.

"Do you think she's always going to be friends with the older kids, Katie?" Renee questioned. There was a narrow, conquering look in Renee's eyes as she asked the question.

Katie was tempted to reply that Renee was her friend, and she was older; but she didn't say anything.

She was very thankful when the bell rang, and they could enter the building. Esther went in ahead of them and sat quietly at her desk.

"Come over to my desk, Katie," said Renee. "We can review the harder words really quick."

Katie watched Esther as she studied her spelling book. "Uh—not right now, Renee."

Katie walked to Esther's desk and stood for a moment. "Hi."

Esther slowly raised her eyes. Her face seemed tiny and distant with the light blond hair wisping around her pink cheeks. "Hi."

"You all ready for the spelling bee?"

Esther shrugged. "Are you?"

"I think so. I studied a lot for it."

Esther nodded as if she already knew that Katie had studied with Renee. She looked down at her word list.

"How's everybody at your house?" Katie asked.

"Okay." Esther's head remained bent over the book. Her voice sounded hard.

"You want to come over again soon?" Katie asked.

Esther shrugged.

"Today or tomorrow?" Katie prodded.

Still Esther made no reply.

"Well?" said Katie impatiently.

Esther looked up at Katie with cold blue eyes, and Katie felt her heart sink. "All you want to do is go to Renee's house and play with her things. You don't like me anymore, and I don't care if we ever play together again as long as I live." Esther was almost shouting.

Katie's face grew warm. She wanted to cry. But she felt Renee's eyes on her, and she gritted her teeth. Some friend Esther was—to say all those nasty things to her.

"Well, I don't care either!" Katie turned and marched to her desk.

"All right, boys and girls," said Mrs. Tuttle after the class had pledged their allegiance to the flag. "We're going to start off with the spelling bee today because

I know you're all looking forward to it. Besides, we're having art class with Miss Carmichael this afternoon, and we have much to do."

Mrs. Tuttle had everyone line up around the room in a circle.

"Quiet, children, so we can begin. Everyone remember how the spelling bee goes? You must say the word before and after you spell it. All right, let's begin."

Joel Kirby got out first, and then Corey Shark. Tracy got out on *pantry* because she spelled it with an *ie* instead of *y*. She plopped down in her desk while some of the kids snickered. Katie smiled at her, hoping she would feel better.

"That's okay, Tracy," said Mrs. Tuttle. "Some of these words are difficult. Now, who's next? Esther, the next word is *loyalty*. Loyalty is a necessary part of friendship."

Katie flushed. So did Esther. Katie wondered if Esther were sorry that she had said all those things to her. Katie almost hoped she would get out. Maybe then she'd be sorry.

Esther swallowed before saying in her quiet voice, "Loyalty. L—o—y—u—l—t—y. Loyalty."

"I'm sorry, Esther, but that's incorrect," said Mrs. Tuttle. "You may sit down with the others."

But Katie didn't feel happy that Esther had gotten out, after all. It was only the first round, and Esther was usually a good speller. Katie tried to catch her eye after she sat down, but Esther just looked at her desk top.

Jillian got Esther's word and spelled it right. Renee gave her a big smile.

It was Katie's turn next. "*Icicles,*" said Mrs. Tuttle. "We hardly ever have icicles in October."

Katie spelled it correctly and smiled to herself. She hoped it would snow soon so that she could build a snowman.

A few more kids got out before it was Renee's turn. "Renee, your word is *handicapped.* Handicapped people need to be loved very much."

Katie felt a little embarrassed—almost as if her parents were standing there giving her another talk. But then she looked at Renee, who was staring at Mrs. Tuttle. Red crept up Renee's neck and over her whole face. All the children stared at Renee.

Then Renee's eyes snapped and she stood up straight, chin out. "Handicapped," she said crisply, without pausing before she spelled out the letters. It seemed as though she had seen that word every day of her life and didn't have to think how to spell it.

"H—a—n—d—i—c—a—p—p—e—d. Handicapped." She spit it out.

Mrs. Tuttle's eyebrows pulled together over the arch in her brown-rimmed glasses. She spoke softly. "Correct. Next round."

Before long, the spelling bee had narrowed down to two people—Katie and Renee. Katie had to spell first.

"Your word is *antique,* Katie," said Mrs. Tuttle. "The old bed in my room is an antique."

The class was perfectly quiet while Katie thought. She pictured her dad's shop next to her house. The red painted letters on the front window read, "Will Paint, Stain, and Upholster. Furniture and Antiques."

"Antique," she repeated steadily. "A—n—t—i—q—u—e. Antique."

When Mrs. Tuttle said, "Correct," several of the children clapped. It made Katie feel like an actress at a curtain call. Her dad would be proud that she had spelled *antique.*

"Renee, spell *deceit,*" said Mrs. Tuttle. "Even 'white lies' are a form of deceit."

"Deceit. D—e—c—e—i—t. Deceit."

Katie sighed. Nothing seemed hard for Renee.

The next word was *discern.* "We need to discern the difference between good and bad," said Mrs. Tuttle. Katie spelled it wrong, and so did Renee.

The class breathed in unison. Both girls were still in. Katie thought she saw Esther watching her.

Katie and Renee each spelled two more rounds successfully before Mrs. Tuttle gave *superstitious* to Katie. "Some people are superstitious about Friday the thirteenth," she said.

"Superstitious. S—u—p—e—r—" Katie breathed deeply. She wasn't sure how it went. "—s—t—i—t—o—u—s. Superstitious."

"I'm sorry, that's incorrect," said Mrs. Tuttle with a sympathetic smile.

Katie let out a breath. Her heart felt hollow. She had wanted to win so badly! She looked to Esther, hoping that Esther would smile at her the way she used to smile whenever Katie was upset about something.

But Esther was staring out the window. Katie felt like crying again.

Mrs. Tuttle had continued with the spelling bee. "Renee, can you spell *superstitious?*"

Renee smiled at Mrs. Tuttle. "Superstitious. S—u—p—e—r—s—t—i—t—i—o—u—s. Superstitious."

"That's correct. Now Renee, you must spell the next word correctly to win the spelling bee. Otherwise, Katie will get another turn. Renee, your word is *gratitude.* Gratitude is important to every friendship."

Renee spelled it right.

Smiling, Mrs. Tuttle said, "Congratulations, Renee. You have won the class spelling bee. Katie, you did a very good job too."

Katie bowed her head and looked at the floor. Her heart sank into her shoes. And she felt as if she were the only one in the whole room.

Then Renee came up to Katie and smiled. "It's a good thing for me that you missed *superstitious,*" she said, "because I wasn't positive how to spell it."

"Oh," said Katie, wishing school were over so that she could go home.

For the first time in her life, Katie didn't care about going to art class and seeing Miss Carmichael. And she didn't care about working on her picture for the art contest.

Chapter Seven

In the Shop

Katie had looked forward to going home that afternoon and getting a hug from her mom.

As she walked toward Maple Lane, a lonely, howling wind came out of the northwest with a fierce whistle. It pounded into her back and sent sharp chills through her whole body. The ends of her hair whipped into her eyes, stinging them.

But no one was there when Katie opened the back door. She went in and set her book bag on the kitchen table. Then she dropped into a chair. Today had been the longest day in her life. She had barely talked to anyone all day. Esther hadn't wanted to talk to her, and she hadn't wanted to talk to Renee.

Katie took a few chocolate chip cookies out of the cookie jar and poured herself a glass of milk.

The kitchen looked strange without her mom in it. The whole house was quiet, except for the wind outside shaking the trees and rattling the front windows.

Katie finished her snack and went upstairs to change into play clothes. Then she put on her old blue coat that she always wore when she helped her dad. She ran out the back door and down the little sidewalk to his shop at the end of the driveway.

Her dad's shop was in a brick one-story building that had been a stable when the house had been built many years before. Mr. Crawford had reroofed it, bricked in the front, and put in new windows. Katie's mom always said that he should have just torn it down and started over, but he said it was against his nature to destroy an antique.

Katie couldn't help noticing the red block letters on his shop window: "Will Paint, Stain, and Upholster. Furniture and Antiques." She sighed and opened the door.

The bell on the door jingled as she pushed it open, but her dad didn't call to her. Katie could hear his lathe humming in the back room. She rubbed her nose, which itched from the strong odor of varnish.

Katie walked around the counter, shuffling through the sprinkling of white sawdust on the floor, past her dad's big upholstery sewing machine. She hoped he needed to upholster something today. She liked to watch the big needle go up and down through the thick fabric.

Under the counter near the door, Mr. Crawford had pretty fabric sample books that Katie often looked through—lush, velvety materials and silky ones, some with flowers printed on them. Some books had only samples of plaid and checked material. Even though they weren't soft to touch, she liked those too.

She picked her way through the chairs and tables tagged for pickup. In a back corner of the shop, rickety furniture pieces sat piled on top of one another, forgotten by their owners.

Katie stood in the doorway of the back room for a moment, watching the abrading tool skim over a stick of wood as it turned on the lathe. She watched the wood spit sawdust away from the machine. It floated above her dad's head and hovered beneath the hanging lamp. Mr. Crawford didn't notice her until he was finished with the wood.

"Oh, hi, Princess! Home from school already?"

She nodded. "What are you making?"

"Spindles for that Windsor settee over there. See how many are missing?" He pointed to a long, pea-green bench with a curved back.

Katie noticed a stack of slightly curved spindles on the work counter near him. "Are you going to paint those new spindles green like the bench?"

"Nope. I'm going to strip the old bench, put in the spindles, and then stain the whole thing in an oak finish."

"I'll bet it'll be pretty," she said, walking over to it.

"Sure will. Come sit up here on your stool and watch me. Then we'll go in and have some cookies, okay?"

She climbed up on her stool in the corner. It was a black-painted stool with gold stenciling on it. "I already had some," she said.

He winked at her. "So did I, but I won't tell if you won't."

Her dad put another stick of wood on the lathe. "Say," he said, pausing, "how'd my girl do in the spelling bee today?"

She looked at the floor and shrugged.

He came over to her and lifted up her chin with his rough, dusty hand. "I take it you didn't win?"

"No." Then Katie began to cry. She remembered standing up in front of the whole class, with Renee next to her smiling triumphantly, and Mrs. Tuttle saying, "Congratulations, Renee. You have won the class spelling bee." She remembered feeling like the loneliest person in the world.

"What happened?" Mr. Crawford bent down so that he was looking directly into her eyes.

Katie gave a long sniff. "R-r-renee won. Sh-sh-she knew everything."

"You're not jealous, are you?" He dabbed at her eyes with the corner of his work apron.

"N-no—not really." Katie sniffed again. "It was her and me for the longest time, and I missed *superstitious,* and she got it."

"I'll bet I couldn't spell *superstitious,* either, Princess; so don't feel bad. It's only a spelling bee, and you can't win every year." He pulled a handkerchief from his back pocket and handed it to her.

Katie blew her nose and continued. "I know. One of my first words was *antique,* Daddy, and I spelled it right because I remembered your shop window."

"Good girl!" He gave her a kiss. "How'd our friend Esther do?"

Katie looked at his rumpled shirt collar. "She got out on the first round."

"Oh, that's too bad."

"Yes, I know. She got out right after Tracy and Joel."

Mr. Crawford was silent. Katie could tell that he was waiting for her to continue.

"Sh-she missed *loyalty*. Sh-she missed it b-because sh-she was mad at me." Katie gave a loud sniff.

"Mad at you?" he repeated.

"W-we had a f-fight before school. She doesn't want to play with me or talk to me anymore—for the whole rest of her life!"

Mr. Crawford pulled her into his arms and held her for a while. "Now that doesn't sound like the Esther I know. Don't you talk to her?"

"Y-yes."

"How much do you talk to Renee?"

Katie hung her head. "A lot. But I'd talk to Esther more if she'd talk to me."

"Hmm. You could work a little harder on that, don't you think? You should also apologize for making her mad. And I doubt that Esther meant what she said about never playing with you again."

Just then the bell jingled on the shop door. There was a sharp click of heels and a voice called, "Is there a Mr. Crawford in here? And how 'bout a little girl?"

Mr. Crawford grinned at Katie, and she wiped her eyes. Then her mom peeked her head in the back doorway and smiled at them.

"I missed you today," Mr. Crawford told her.

Mrs. Crawford gave them each a kiss.

Katie slipped her arms around her mother's waist and buried her face in her coat. Mrs. Crawford held her a while before asking quietly, "Who won the spelling bee, honey?"

Her answer was muffled, but Mrs. Crawford understood it.

"Have you been crying about it?" she asked.

Another sob rose in Katie's throat, and she nodded.

"You didn't play with anyone this afternoon?"

"No, she's been out here with me," said Mr. Crawford.

"R-renee wanted to play today after her violin lesson, but I—I didn't feel like it." Katie sniffed and pulled away from her mother. She began to walk toward the front of the shop. "I—I wanted to play with Esther. I mean, I thought she might want to play with me—anyway, sh-she didn't, and—and I walked home alone."

The shop felt big and empty, with the cold cement floor under her feet and the wind knocking on the front door. Leaves blew past the windows. Katie dug her hands into the pockets of her blue coat and pulled it closely around her. She wondered what Esther had done that afternoon. She wondered if Esther wished that they had played together.

Through the shop window Katie could see the Greshams' house across the street beneath the rocking oaks and maples. She could see a warm glow in the side kitchen window. Esther was probably setting the table for supper. Katie wondered what she had told Mrs. Gresham about the spelling bee.

"So what do you two want for supper? I've only got leftover roast beef or tuna hotdish. I need to go to the grocery tomorrow." Mrs. Crawford came up behind Katie and drew her back into a warm embrace.

"Can we order a pizza instead?" Katie asked.

"We really need to eat up those leftovers before I go to the grocery."

"Come on, Jayne," said Mr. Crawford. "Let Katie order a pizza."

"Pizza!" exclaimed Jeffers, on his way into the shop. "That'd be great! I'm starved. Football practice was really tough today with the wind blowing so hard."

"Please, Mom!"

Mrs. Crawford laughed. "All right, I give in. Somebody order a pizza."

Katie pulled away from her mother and ran with Jeffers to the shop counter. They took out the phone directory and dialed the number.

Mrs. Crawford glanced absently around the shop. "Alan," she said, "what are you going to do with all these leftover furniture pieces?"

"You mean the ones nobody's claimed?"

"Yes—like that rocker over there and this table that doesn't have any chairs."

He looked at her suspiciously. "Where do you think you're going to put them?"

"Not for us, Alan. For the Center. I think it could use some homey furniture. You know, the things the government sends are so modern-looking."

Mr. Crawford rubbed his hand over his eyes. "But that furniture has to be fixed up, and I'm too busy with all of my Christmas orders."

"You wouldn't have to do it. We could all pitch in and do it together," she suggested.

"Well, if there's any sawing to do, I want to do it," Jeffers declared.

"I want to paint," said Katie.

"You see?" said Mrs. Crawford. "It would be a good experience for the children."

"Okay," Mr. Crawford agreed. "When do you want to start?"

"Let's start right now!" said Katie.

Mr. Crawford laughed. "You're as bad as your mother."

"What can I have?" Mrs. Crawford asked.

"Anything in that back corner. That's all been here too long to be claimed. I honestly don't know what you're going to find, Jayne. Most of it needs a lot of work. That table, for example. One of the legs is shorter than the others—I was going to put a new leg on it."

"Can't we just saw the legs off so they're a couple feet high? It would be a good drawing table for the children."

"Are there a lot of small children there, Mom?" asked Katie.

"Yes—several are five or six years old."

"Are all the children like Louis?"

"No," said Mrs. Crawford. "Some have more disabilities. And some have less—especially the little ones."

"They're cuter when they're little," said Katie. "Somehow, older ones are more scary."

"Katie!" said Mrs. Crawford. "We don't like people because they look cute or scary. How would you like it if someone thought you were scary?"

"But I'm not," said Katie.

"And neither are they," Mrs. Crawford answered. She walked over to her husband and asked quietly, "Alan, what do you think about Katie coming to the Center, say once a week, to help us with the children?"

Katic stared at her parents in surprise.

"Sounds like a good idea," said Mr. Crawford. "Katie, what do you think?"

She wrinkled her nose a little. That didn't sound like a very exciting way to spend her afternoons. "What would I have to do?"

"Oh, read to them and play with them," said Mrs. Crawford. "Nothing awful. I think you'd enjoy it. It'll give you something to do on afternoons when you're not playing with anyone."

Katie made no response. She was thinking about how she had no one to play with anymore.

"Will you come once a week, Katie?" her mother asked.

Katie looked at her parents. "Yes, I guess so."

"Good girl," said her father. "Jeffers, how 'bout helping me with this furniture?"

Jeffers and his dad pulled the table out so that they could work on it. Katie followed her mom as she tiptoed between the piles. There were clocks without faces and cabinets without doors. Springs jutted through ripped seat cushions. Mrs. Crawford took a good look at every piece of furniture.

"You'd better go in and change," said her husband.

"Yes, and I suppose I'd better work on a salad while I'm in there. Jeffers, you go change too, if you're going to work out here tonight."

Mr. Crawford switched off the light in the back room. "We might as well all go in until the pizza comes. Katie, come set the table for your mother."

Jeffers left and ran to the house while Katie picked her way out of the furniture. Mr. and Mrs. Crawford began walking across the yard. Katie hurried to catch up.

"So you had a good day?" Mr. Crawford said to his wife.

"Yes, very. The children are adorable. And they so much want to be loved. I'm afraid most of them haven't gotten enough attention at home."

"None of them gave you a hard time?"

"Oh, no. Well, some of the adults are pretty strong-willed but not bad. They'll learn to obey. Eda Williams is in charge of the Center, you know. She always has a firm hand."

"That's good. She's a patient woman. How was Louis today?"

"Excited as I've ever seen him. You know, he calls it 'his' school. He kept quite busy telling everyone else what to do. He also latched onto a new little boy named Robbie whose father brought him as soon as we got there—I guess before he went to work. It was sad to see the father, Alan."

"Why?"

"He was embarrassed about Robbie. Couldn't wait to leave him with us."

"And what's Robbie like?" asked Mr. Crawford.

"He's Down's syndrome like Louis. I asked the father about him, but he didn't tell me too much. I don't think the family works well with him."

Chapter Eight

After-School Lessons

"Hey, Katie," said Renee when the final bell rang one bleak Thursday in November. "Want a sucker? I've got a whole bunch of them today. I've been giving everybody one, but I guess I'll give you more since you're going to be the star of the Thanksgiving program."

Katie blushed happily. She was playing Priscilla Alden in the Pilgrim play—the part that all the girls had wanted. "It's going to be a lot of fun, isn't it? I'm glad you got a part in the play too, Renee."

Renee shrugged. "I don't care about the play, anyway. I'm playing a violin solo in the program, and that's a lot harder than being in a dumb old play. I'll have to practice my violin solo almost every day after school. That's why they gave me a smaller part in the play, you know."

"Oh," said Katie. Somehow she didn't feel quite so excited about her part in the play now.

Renee held out two suckers to her. "Here, take a lemon and an orange. I'm eating all the strawberry and grape ones 'cause they're my favorites."

They were Katie's favorites too, but she didn't say anything. She unwrapped the orange one and gave it a big lick.

"Want to come over today?" continued Renee. "We haven't played for a long time."

Katie began stuffing her books and papers into her book bag. She would be glad to get home and warm up. There was a cold draft sliding in between the window frame and the windowsill near her desk.

It would be a perfect day to put on a play. Katie wished she had asked Esther to come over so they could rehearse their lines for the play. It seemed like their lines in the Pilgrim play were the only words they had said to each other since the spelling bee.

"Yeah, I'll come over," Katie answered. "But I'll have to call my mom from your house and tell her where I am so she can pick me up after work."

Renee seemed to fidget with her books as she listened to Katie talk. "What time would she pick you up?" she asked hesitantly.

"Oh, about half-past five," said Katie, walking toward the classroom door. "You ready to go?"

"Umm—" stammered Renee, "I forgot; I can't play today after all. I need to practice my violin."

"For two hours?" asked Katie.

"Well, I have to practice for the Thanksgiving program. I want to make sure Mom and Dad will be proud of me."

"Oh." Katie was puzzled. "Then I guess we can play some other day."

Since Renee couldn't play with her, Katie decided to go to the Center. She left Jefferson Elementary and walked down Chestnut Street. By going this way she wouldn't have to meet Esther. It seemed like years since Katie and Esther had slid down the oak banister on the Greshams' staircase or played dolls in Esther's room.

The sky was stark white with streaks of dismal gray stretching over the tops of the trees. Only a few leaves were left dangling from the tree branches on Chestnut Street. The rest littered the lawns and sidewalks.

The wind tossed the leaves into Katie's face. She wrapped her scarf around her neck and plunged her hand into her coat pocket. But the wind even whipped through her coat.

It felt as if it would snow. Katie hoped it would snow because her birthday was coming on Saturday.

Off Chestnut was Birch Street, where the Center was. Katie ran down the sidewalk toward the long one-story brick building with the little orange school bus parked in front of it.

When Katie entered the building, she stepped onto a thick doormat and began to take off her scarf and mittens. A radiator vent near the front door was sending out hot air. Katie stood over the vent and let the heat shoot up her legs.

Inside, there were different rooms for each of the groups at the Center. Katie could see the adults having classes and making crafts in the rooms on her left. All the children were playing in the long playroom to her right. The playroom had a wall of windows looking out onto the street.

A few children were drawing at the low table from Mr. Crawford's shop. Most of the children played alone, talking to dolls or trucks or just to themselves. Right away Katie spotted Louis pulling a brown-haired boy across the room. Louis stopped once and gave him a bear hug. Katie was afraid Louis would squash him, but the boy emerged smiling.

Katie looked at her mother, who was reading to a girl on her lap. Jealousy stabbed at Katie's heart. She wanted to run over and push that girl off. What right had she to be sitting on Mom's lap? If she wanted to sit on a mother's lap, she should go home. Maybe Katie wanted to sit there today. The girl would have to get off.

The girl was too big to be sitting there anyway. Her legs hung almost to the floor. She was drooling a little and wiping it on her shirt front. Katie thought it was disgusting.

"Hi, honey." Mrs. Crawford looked up and smiled at Katie. "I'm glad you're here. Come over and meet Krissy. She's ten years old."

Katie would be ten on Saturday. She glanced at the book Mrs. Crawford was reading to Krissy. It was Beatrix Potter's *Peter Rabbit.* She had read that in first grade.

Katie hesitated. What if Krissy hit her? Sometimes disabled children did those things.

Mrs. Crawford wiped Krissy's mouth and said, "Katie, come here please."

Katie went to them reluctantly. "Hi, Krissy," she said.

Krissy stared at her.

"Krissy," said Mrs. Crawford, "this is my girl, Katie. She lives at my house with me."

Krissy eyed Katie. Katie plunged her hands into her coat pockets. She felt the other sucker that Renee had given her. She wished she had gone home and eaten her sucker in peace instead of coming to the Center.

"Remember, Krissy doesn't know you," Mrs. Crawford told Katie.

Katie thought for a second, and then pulled out the lemon sucker. "Here, Krissy. Want a sucker?"

Krissy grabbed it. Her eyes grew wide, and she made a strange sound in her throat. Her fingers fumbled with the wrapper.

Katie took the sucker back.

"No!" Krissy said, clawing for it.

"I'm just going to unwrap it for you," Katie explained. "See?" She ripped off the top of the plastic wrapper and pulled the sucker out. "Now you can have it back."

Krissy stuffed the whole thing in her mouth and began sucking and drooling.

Mrs. Crawford helped her take the sucker back out of her mouth. "Say 'thank you,' " she reminded her.

Krissy's mouth began to form the words. "Th-thank 'ou."

"You're welcome," said Katie.

Krissy smiled at her. Her smile was wide and curved, and it put dimples into her cheeks. She looked pleasant now. Katie wasn't afraid of her anymore.

"Ka-tie!" Louis hollered from across the room. "Ka-tie!"

"Louis, what are you up to?" Katie asked, walking over to him.

He put his hands on his hips and tossed his head. "Goofin' up."

Katie laughed. "You mean 'goofing around'?"

"Yeah, goofin' aroun'."

Katie looked at the little brown-haired boy next to Louis. The little boy was panting from having run all around the room.

He was very short—short enough to be three or four years old—but he looked older. He had squinty green eyes and long, straight lashes. One of his eyes rested near his nose while the other looked curiously around the room. He had round, soft cheeks with a spot of pink on each one, a flat little nose that turned up at the end, and a very small mouth.

"What's your name?" she asked him.

He blinked at her. "Rrr-robbie," he said in a scared voice.

Katie squatted in front of him. She had never thought that a disabled child might be afraid of her.

"Don't be scared, Robbie," she said. "My name is Katie. How would you like me to read you a story?"

He nodded.

"Me too," said Louis.

"All right," said Katie, "but you have to be quiet during the story."

He put his fingers on his lips and said, "Shhh."

"Good. Okay, let's go over and sit on that big couch. Grab that book on the floor, Louis, and I'll read it to you," Katie said.

Robbie began to climb up onto her lap. Katie took a breath. She really didn't want him sitting on her. But Mrs. Crawford was watching, and so Katie pulled him up. Louis patted her knees. "Hold me," he whined.

"Louis, you're too big to hold," Katie answered. "You're bigger than me."

"Hold me, too!"

"Louis, you're a big boy, and big boys don't need to be held. Robbie is just a little boy."

"Big boy," said Louis, throwing back his shoulders and sitting on the sofa next to her.

Katie opened the storybook. It was about Paul Bunyan. Katie began to read: " 'Once upon a time there was a huge baby born in the state of Maine whose name was Paul Bunyan.' "

"Paul Dung-eon?" Louis repeated.

"No, Bunyan, Louis. He was the biggest lumberjack in America—probably the biggest person ever!" said Katie. "But he's really just a pretend person because no one could be that big."

"I'm big," said Louis, looking down at his stomach.

Katie laughed. "I know you are. You're a lot bigger than me and Robbie. But you never caused all the problems that Paul Bunyan did when he was born." Katie showed Louis and Robbie a picture of Paul lying in a forest, as large as the trees, wearing a diaper as big as a house.

" 'When Paul wiggled his toes he knocked down four miles of forest,' " Katie read. " 'So the people in Maine asked him to move to Minnesota.' "

"I live Minne-sota," said Louis, pointing to himself.

"So do I," said Katie. " 'In Minnesota Paul grew so big that his mother could hardly find clothes for him to wear. She had to use wagon wheels for his buttons.' "

"Wheels?" said Louis. "Vroom! Vroom!" He put his hands on an imaginary motorcycle and turned the handles.

" 'Paul ate forty bowls of porridge every morning for breakfast—' "

"Breakfas'!" exclaimed Louis. "I like pancakes."

"Well, Paul didn't get pancakes. He had porridge. It's hot cereal that tastes like glue."

"Yum, yum." Louis licked his lips.

"You're crazy," said Katie, laughing. "Now be quiet and let me finish the story. 'On Paul's first birthday, his parents gave him a blue ox named Babe.' That's like a cow," Katie explained.

"Moo," said Louis.

" 'Babe was only half as big as Paul, but he was still bigger than five elephants put together. Paul loved his birthday present.' "

"I like birthdays," said Louis.

"Me too," Katie answered, smiling. "My birthday's in two days. Did you know that?"

"Happy Birthday," said Louis.

"Thank you. Robbie, when's your birthday?"

Robbie just looked at her.

"Mine's tomorrow," said Louis.

"No, it's not," said Katie. "Yours is in the summer."

"Oh, yeah. I forgot."

"If you're not quiet I can't finish this," Katie warned. "Now, 'Paul and Babe helped the lumberjacks in Minnesota by making more waterways. They walked through the whole state, putting their footprints into the ground. When it rained, the prints filled up with water and formed 10,000 lakes.' "

Katie showed them a picture of Paul making lakes with his feet. Then she turned the page. " 'When Paul was grown up, he ate a lot more than porridge. He ate pancakes as big as swimming pools. The griddle was so big that on a foggy day, you couldn't see across it. The cooks had to skate around the griddle with bacon tied to their feet just to keep it greased.' "

"Pancakes!" shouted Louis, looking at the picture of the big griddle and rubbing his stomach. "I'm hungry."

"You're always hungry," said Katie. "Now listen to the ending. 'Before long, Paul had chopped down so many trees in Minnesota that—' "

"You having a birthday party?" Louis asked.

Katie paused, and then said reluctantly, "Uh-huh."

"I'm coming?" he asked, raising his eyebrows.

"Uh—" Katie glanced away. "Let's finish the story, Louis. Then we'll talk about the party."

"I'm coming?" he repeated.

"Louis, you can't come. It's a costume party. That means we all dress up like storybook characters. You don't have a costume, do you?"

He frowned. "What's your cos-tume?"

Katie smiled a little as she pictured it. "I'm going to be Dorothy from *The Wizard of Oz*."

Louis thought for a minute. "I have cos-tume. Now I come? Please come?" Louis tugged on her sleeve.

Katie thought of Renee. She wouldn't like it. She didn't like to be around Louis. She didn't even want Tracy to come, let alone Louis.

"But it's going to be all girls," Katie told him. "No boys."

"Good," said Louis. "I like girls."

"Don't you like boys?"

"No." He looked at the floor and frowned. His round lip formed into a pout.

"Why not?"

A tear squeezed out of one eye. " 'Cause."

"Because why, Louis?" Katie put down the book.

Another tear fell, and he sniffed loudly. "They call me rrr-retard."

Katie was silent.

"It's bad to be rrr-retard?" he looked at her through blurry eyes.

"No, Louis," said Katie gently. "It's not bad at all. You're extra special, and God loves you very much."

"Do you love me?"

Katie smiled at him tenderly, and her heart thumped. "Of course I do. And you can come to my birthday party and eat lots of cake and ice cream."

"Yum, yum!"

Katie looked up and found that Mrs. Crawford was smiling at her. Katie smiled back.

"Yea!" shouted Louis. "I'm going to birthday party! Cake and ice cream! No boys!"

"Shhh," said Katie. "Or everybody will want to come. Let me finish the story."

Robbie snuggled against her. His round face touched hers as she bent over to read the book. Robbie felt very warm in her lap. Louis put his arm around her shoulders.

"Louis," Katie said. "Don't do that."

"But I love you. You're my friend."

"Thank you, Louis. You're mine too."

The front door of the Center opened, and the cold air rushed into the playroom. Several parents had arrived for their children. Mrs. Williams and Mrs. Crawford collected coats and mittens and sent the children off with their parents.

Then Katie's mother came over to the sofa. "Robbie, Daddy's here to get you."

Robbie snuggled closer to Katie.

A tall, thin man with graying hair entered the room. He looked very pale, with a long white neck and face. He even had a long nose and dark-rimmed glasses that slid toward the end of it. His eyes ran over the room until he noticed Robbie.

"Time to go," he said in a quiet voice.

Katie lifted Robbie off her lap. He walked slowly toward his father.

"I hope he wasn't too much trouble for you," the man said to Mrs. Crawford.

"Oh, no—not at all. He's perfectly obedient."

"I appreciate your working with him," continued the man. "I know it must get tiring. My wife and I hardly know where to start. We get so discouraged."

Mrs. Crawford's eyebrows pulled together, putting lines in her forehead. "I've found that it's only discouraging when I expect too much. But when we accept each child for who he is, and love that child, then everything he learns is a reward."

He sighed and gave her a weak smile. "I'm afraid it's not that simple when it's your child and you've planned so many great things for him before he was born. You expect so much. And then he's born like this, and you realize none of it will ever happen."

Mrs. Crawford shook her head. "Naturally, it's discouraging when you look at it that way."

The man didn't answer. He put Robbie's coat and mittens on him and guided him out of the Center. Katie and Louis went to the window and watched them drive away.

The wind was still blowing the tree branches, but there weren't many leaves left, even on the ground. Every so often, a tiny drop of water dabbed the windowpane and trickled down to the sill.

Katie squinted to see the rain coming down. She saw only a graying sky and a dark row of trees that lined the wet street.

"Snow!" shouted Louis, smudging the window with his nose.

"No, it's rain, Louis, not snow," said Katie.

But as she looked, she could see little white flakes settling on the withered grass.

Chapter Nine

Snow Day

"Mom," Katie asked that night when she was helping her mom put away the clean supper dishes, "where's that box of costumes that Esther and I always used for our plays?"

Mrs. Crawford's eyebrows rose, and she smiled. "Are you and Esther going to get together to act out another play?"

"Not exactly," Katie said. "I got the part of Priscilla Alden in the Thanksgiving program! It's the very most important girls' part. I even have the first line in the play. I'm not married to John Alden yet, and I'm helping to get Thanksgiving ready. I say, 'I hope we have enough sweet potatoes fixed. John loves them so.' "

"Good for you!" exclaimed her mother, giving her a hug.

"Nate Wainwright is John Alden. At least he's better than Barry or Joel. Barry's going to be Squanto—he says he's going to scalp the Pilgrims at the Thanksgiving dinner. And he better not! He'll ruin the whole play."

Mrs. Crawford smiled again.

"Anyway, Mom, we have to find our own costumes, and I was wondering if we had anything that I could wear."

"I think the box is in the attic, but I doubt if there's anything that you can use. I think this play calls for a real costume—a brand-new one. What do you think?"

"That'd be great!"

"I have to go shopping tomorrow, so I'll pick up some material. We'll make you one with a big white collar, and an apron too."

"I don't know if you'll be shopping tomorrow or not, Jayne," said Mr. Crawford, coming in from the living room. "The snow is coming down hard now, and we're in for about a thirty-mile-an-hour wind tonight and tomorrow morning."

"Brrr!" said Mrs. Crawford, shivering.

Katie ran to the kitchen window and looked out. Snow was falling in sheets through the black sky and swirling past the windows.

"Does that mean we won't have to go to school tomorrow?" shouted Jeffers from the living room.

Mr. Crawford laughed. "Could be. I'd really rather you didn't go out," he said to his wife. "It'll be dangerous, and I doubt if they'll be opening up the Center anyway."

"But I *have* to go out," she said distinctly, as she raised her eyebrows and looked at him.

"Can't whatever you have to get wait one day?"

"No," she said slowly so he would understand, "I can't get it the next day. That's the day of Katie's party."

"Ohh," he said, smiling. "I get it."

Katie turned around and looked at them. "You haven't gotten my birthday present yet?"

Mrs. Crawford threw a glance at her husband.

"You think we would tell you?" her dad responded.

Katie laughed. "No. I hope you remember what I asked for."

"We already told you that the town house was very expensive, honey," said Mrs. Crawford.

Katie sighed. "Yes, I know."

Mr. and Mrs. Crawford glanced at each other again as Mr. Crawford took the Bible off the kitchen counter. "How 'bout if everybody assembles in the living room for devotions tonight?" he said. "I'll make up a fire."

"That'd be nice, dear," said Mrs. Crawford. "Now, Katie," she continued, "would you like a little Pilgrim cap too? And what color do you want the dress to be?"

"Miss Lauren said that the girls playing mothers should wear gray or brown, but that I could wear blue, because Priscilla was young. She sent a note home with me today telling you all about the costumes."

"After devotions I want you to go get it so that I can take it shopping with me tomorrow," said Mrs. Crawford.

Mrs. Crawford and Katie went into the living room and sat down near the fireplace. Jeffers was lying on his stomach on the floor. After the fire caught, Mr. Crawford sat down in the big blue armchair.

"Okay," he said. "Tonight we're in Mark 9 as we work our way through the Gospels. Verses 33 through 37. See if this passage sounds familiar."

Katie watched the flames snap at the kindling and lick the logs while Mr. Crawford read:

> And he came to Capernaum: and being in the house he asked them, What was it that ye disputed among yourselves by the way?

> But they held their peace: for by the way they had disputed among themselves, who should be the greatest.
>
> And he sat down, and called the twelve, and saith unto them, If any man desire to be first, the same shall be last of all, and servant of all.
>
> And he took a child, and set him in the midst of them: and when he had taken him in his arms, he said unto them,
>
> Whosoever shall receive one of such children in my name, receiveth me: and whosoever shall receive me, receiveth not me, but him that sent me.

Mr. Crawford looked up at his family. "Remember when we read the parallel passage in Matthew? What did it mean? Do you remember?"

Katie and Jeffers stared at the fire. Finally, Katie said, "It meant that we have to be nice to little children because God loves them."

"Yes, it meant that," agreed Mr. Crawford. "What else? What does pride have to do with being kind to children? Why did Jesus say all of this right after the disciples bragged about who was the greatest?"

Katie and Jeffers didn't answer. Katie was remembering how she hadn't wanted to go near Krissy at the Center that day. She wondered if she had been proud.

Mr. Crawford watched his children intently for a moment before he said, "I wonder if you two brag to your friends at school. Jeffers, what about winning your last football game? And Katie, I heard you tell your mother that you got an important part in the Thanksgiving play. I hope you kids don't feel proud about the things you do, even if you can do them well. Jesus is telling his disciples here that they need to become humble—like little children. Let's remember that we're not more important than anyone else, okay?"

Katie and Jeffers nodded.

Mr. Crawford smiled at them, and his eyes sparkled. "Katie, your mother told me that you visited the Center today and that you were very kind to Louis and his new friend. I'm proud of you, Princess."

She smiled. "It was more fun than I thought it would be."

"Kindnesses always are," said Mrs. Crawford, and she reached over and squeezed Katie's hand.

Then Mr. Crawford closed their devotions in prayer, and Mrs. Crawford shooed Katie and Jeffers upstairs to do their homework.

As Katie walked down the hallway, she heard the phone ring.

Snatches of Mrs. Crawford's conversation carried up the stairs. "Oh, really? . . . that bad, huh? . . . Well, thank you, Eda. Be sure to call me back if anything changes. . . . What?" Then she laughed. "Yes, she enjoyed it, too. . . . Thank you. I'm glad he had fun with her too. . . . Oh, yes, he's more than welcome to come to the party. . . . That would be darling! He thought of that himself? . . . Oh, I see. . . . No, I won't tell Katie. Okay, Bye-bye."

"Was that Mrs. Williams?" Katie shouted.

"Yes."

"What did she say about my party?"

Mrs. Crawford was chuckling to herself. "She said Louis is ready to come over right now. He's so excited! I'm glad you invited him, honey."

Mr. and Mrs. Crawford walked up the stairs.

"Do you know what he's dressing up as?" Katie asked.

Her mother smiled. "Can't tell you. It's a secret."

"But there is some news that we can tell you," said Mr. Crawford, his eyes twinkling.

"There's no school!" Katie yelled excitedly.

"No school?" echoed Jeffers, throwing open his bedroom door.

Mrs. Crawford looked at her husband and laughed. "All we know is that the Center will be closed. That doesn't mean your schools will be closed."

"They'd better be!" said Jeffers.

"Can we stay up late and play games?" Katie asked eagerly.

Her parents looked at each other.

"I guess so," said Mr. Crawford with a smile.

"All right!" Katie and Jeffers shouted.

So Mrs. Crawford made popcorn and hot chocolate, and the whole family stayed up until midnight playing games in front of the fire. Katie wished it would snow hard every night so they could stay up.

When Katie awoke the next morning, her room was very bright. She jumped out of bed and put up the window shade. Snow draped the back yard like a white cape, thrown over the bushes and sloping up to the fence. Snow weighted the pine tree branches down to the perfectly covered ground. The yard glistened under the morning sun.

She put on her robe and slippers and ran downstairs to the kitchen.

Mrs. Crawford was sitting at the oak table looking through cookbooks. "Mornin', sleepyhead."

"Mornin', " Katie said.

"Did you see the snow?" she asked.

"Yes, it's beautiful! I can't wait to go out and play! When's Jeffers getting up?"

"Anytime. Dad'll be in soon to get him out to shovel the driveway."

"I guess school was cancelled, wasn't it?" Katie sat down.

Mrs. Crawford got up and cut her a few slices of the banana bread that was cooling on the counter. "Nice and warm," she said. "Yes, they cancelled it at 6:00 this morning. It's still blowing out in the country."

"What are you looking for in those cookbooks?" Katie asked, buttering her bread. She savored each melting bite.

"Party ideas. What kind of cake do you want this year?"

"Butter brickle cake with butter brickle frosting."

"You have that every year."

"But I like it."

Katie and her mother heard the stomping of Mr. Crawford's heavy boots on the back porch. He stepped in and pulled the wet boots off his feet.

"Umm, banana bread," he said with a sniff. He tiptoed over the puddle of water by the door. "There's almost a foot out there!" he announced. "It's a record snowfall for early November, that's for sure."

"Do you think it will all melt, Daddy?" Katie asked.

"Some of it. It's a wet snow, and the sun should come out today and tomorrow. Perfect packing weather." His eyes twinkled boyishly as he walked into the hallway and up the stairs to Jeffers' room.

When he returned to the kitchen, he cut himself some banana bread and sat down. "Katie, how'd you like to help us shovel?"

She could tell that it was more of a command than a request. "Sure, Daddy."

"All right, hurry and get dressed. Jeffers is putting his clothes on now."

Katie ran upstairs and pulled on her warmest play clothes. Her mom had the ski clothes and boots waiting for Katie and Jeffers when they got down to the kitchen.

As Katie and Jeffers went outside, they smelled the crisp, clean, wet scent of newly fallen snow. Katie took in a giant breath of air and dropped into a snowdrift. It was as soft as an overstuffed armchair.

Mr. Crawford had two shovels waiting by the porch, jutting out of the snow. He had already shoveled from the back door to the shop.

"Let's get movin' so we can have some fun," he said.

But he and Jeffers threw a few hard snowballs at one another before they did any work.

The shoveling didn't take too long. Soon Katie and Jeffers had rolled two balls for a snowman in the front yard.

"I think we ought to have a snow family," said Katie as they placed the smaller ball on top of the larger one.

"Yeah," said Jeffers. "Let's do it. We've got enough snow!"

"We could make our family!"

"All right, you keep rolling, and I'll go find all the sticks for their arms," said Jeffers. He took out his pocketknife and ran to the back yard.

Katie rolled all the bottom balls while Jeffers was gone. She lined them up next to the snowman already there. That snowman was pretty big, and so it would be Mr. Crawford. There was a medium-sized ball for

Mrs. Crawford, a smaller one for Jeffers, and a little one for Katie.

As she began rolling the balls for their heads, she noticed the Gresham kids across the street. The boys were helping Pastor Gresham finish the shoveling. The three girls were shoveling the snow off the front porch. Then they all ran into the yard, and Esther began helping them roll balls.

Katie stopped to watch. Jeffers came around the side of their house with a handful of sticks.

"Here're the arms. Why are you just standing there?"

Katie turned back to the snowmen. "Esther's over there."

"Good—they're out!" exclaimed Jeffers, glancing across the street. "I'm going to go play with Matt and Luke." He tossed the sticks on the ground.

"Jeffers!" wailed Katie, running after him and grabbing his ski jacket. "You said you'd play with me."

"I only said I'd cut the sticks." Jeffers loosened her hold on his jacket and pulled away.

"Please play with me," she begged. "I don't want to play by myself." She looked earnestly into his brown eyes. They were round like hers, but his lashes curled out farther. His eyebrows had started getting bushy like their dad's, and his brown hair was blown across his forehead the wrong way.

"Why play with me when you could play with Esther?" he asked.

Katie sat down in the snow and began to break one of Jeffers' twigs. "I can't play with her because she doesn't like me anymore. She never wants to play. We'll never be friends again."

"Sure you will," he answered. "Just look at her over there. She's more lonely than you are. Luke's even told me so."

"Really?"

"Yeah, lots of times. She wants to play again." Jeffers gave her a grin and held out his hand to pull her up. "Go ask her to play. We can all go sledding together when Dad gets the toboggans out."

Katie looked back at Esther standing in the middle of her front yard. "Okay," she said. "Will you come with me?"

"Let's go." Jeffers led the way through the snow that had drifted into the yard and street.

"Hi, Esther!" Katie called when she reached the other curb.

"Hi, Katie." Esther looked surprised to see her.

"Hi, Katie," said everybody else. "Hi, Jeffers."

Pastor Gresham set down his shovel and came over. "Haven't seen you for a while, Katie."

"No, sir," she answered. "I came over to see if Esther wanted to help me make snowmen. Jeffers and I started making our family."

"But I'm ready to start a tunnel," said Jeffers to the boys. Are you almost done shoveling?"

"Go ahead and start the tunnel," said Pastor Gresham. "I'll finish up this last part."

The boys yelled with delight and ran to the back yard.

Katie took a breath and said, "Do you want to come over and help with the snow family, Esther? Sharon and Susanna can come too if they want."

"We're going to make twin snow girls," Sharon said.

"Go ahead, Esther," said Susanna.

Esther smiled. "Okay."

While Katie and Esther rolled the rest of the snow family's heads, Jeffers, Matt, and Luke finished their tunnel.

After lunch Katie and Esther made snow angels in the Crawfords' yard.

Then the children all climbed on their toboggans and went sledding down Maple Lane.

They slid most of the afternoon, starting their toboggans at their houses and coasting down the hill from there, letting the wind tangle their hair. Their cheeks and noses grew pink, and their eyes watered happily. Katie thought that the hill would have been too steep for walking up if the ride down hadn't been so much fun.

All too soon, the snow plows rumbled down Maple Lane and forced the children off the street.

Katie and Esther gathered up the sticks Jeffers had cut and put them in the sides of all the snow family members. They found wood chips around the front bushes and used them for eyes. Mrs. Gresham gave them four carrots for the noses. Then the girls tied a frilly apron around the snow lady for Mrs. Crawford and a work apron around the one for Mr. Crawford. Jeffers' snowman wore a baseball cap.

"I don't know what to put on the snowman that's supposed to be me," said Katie.

Esther dropped into the snow and thought for a minute. "Does your mom have anything for the party yet? Like hats or noisemakers?"

"Yeah, they're in the kitchen."

"We can use those!" said Esther.

"Good idea!" Katie and Esther ran into the kitchen and took one hat and one noisemaker out of the cupboard. The phone began to ring as they closed the door behind them.

Katie returned to answer it.

Esther came in, shut the door, and sat on a kitchen chair to wait.

Katie flushed a little as she answered the voice on the other end. "Umm—yeah, I'm glad there's no school today, too. . . . You're going sledding at the golf course? . . . Sure, I'd love to come! That sounds like fun!—Oh, wait. What time? . . . Now? . . . You see, Esther's here. . . ."

Esther blushed and looked at the floor.

"Well, I don't know. We've just been playing all day. Esther, how long—"

Esther stood up. Her face was red and her mouth was set in a hard line. "I'll just go home, Katie. You can go with Renee."

"No, wait, Esther." Katie blushed too. "I didn't mean it that way. You can come too. We're done with our snowmen now anyway. Renee?" she said into the phone. "Can Esther come too? It'll be fun. . . . We'll just get a ride from someone 'cause my mom is gone with the car. . . . All right, maybe we'll see you there. Maybe we won't." She hung up the phone.

"Are you going?" Esther asked.

"I don't know. What do you want to do? Your mom would have to drive us."

"I'm not going sledding."

"Why not?"

"Because I don't want to," Esther said. Her voice squeaked when she said it.

"You liked it when we went sledding on our street today."

"That was different."

"Why?" said Katie, growing impatient.

"Because it was just us and our brothers and sisters. You know that." Esther opened the door and went outside. "If you want to go sledding with Renee, go ahead."

Esther let the door close by itself. She ran down the porch steps and across the snow-covered yard. Katie ran after her.

"Esther! Wait!" she yelled.

But Esther ran across the street and into her big maroon house.

Katie sat down on the top step of the front porch and rested her face in her mittened hands. Tears glazed her eyes and spread across her eyelashes. She blinked them away.

The sun had begun to set behind the gray trees and houses along Maple Lane, casting long shadows across the snow. The shadows reached over the freezing slush in the street. They crept across the snow angels in Katie's front yard and up to the Crawford snow family. Katie saw through the blur of her tears that her snow girl remained undecorated—separated from all the others.

Chapter Ten

Katie's Birthday Party

Katie had sent out invitations for her party a week early. They were little store-bought invitations with a picture of Mother Goose on the front. She was having a dress-up party, and everybody's costume had to be from a story.

Katie couldn't wait to wear her Dorothy costume. *The Wizard of Oz* was one of her favorite books. And she had seen it on television at least five times.

The morning of her birthday, the first thing Katie did when she got up was try on the ruby slippers her mother had bought her. They were dark red, with shiny red flecks in them. The light blue dress she was going to wear hung from her closet door, crisply ironed. Her mother was also going to braid her hair and put bows in it.

"Good morning, Birthday Girl," Mrs. Crawford's voice said from the doorway.

Katie turned around and smiled. "Hi, Mom."

Mrs. Crawford came in and gave her a hug and a kiss. "How's it feel to be ten years old?"

Katie smiled happily. "Almost the same as being nine, but somehow better." She looked at the clock and sighed.

"I don't think I can wait 'til my party starts this afternoon!"

That morning Katie watched her mother frost her butter brickle cake and set the table with party favors and hats. Katie wondered what everyone would wear and who would come first. Her heart leaped excitedly when the doorbell's ring announced the first arrival.

Katie flung open the door and found Louis there. She sighed and stepped by to let him in.

He was dressed like a scarecrow, with ragged pants and shirt, a tattered straw hat, and hay sticking out from his sleeves and pant legs. He put his arm around Katie's shoulders. "We match," he said, grinning.

"I'm sorry we're early, but I had to get him over here," Mrs. Williams said, coming in behind him. "He was starting to pull out his straw."

Katie looked at Louis again. She wasn't so sure she wanted to match him.

"Louis told me that he had to be like Katie and that she was going to be Dorothy," Mrs. Williams said as she turned to leave. "So I suggested that he be the Scarecrow. I think he looks cute, even if he is itching. Maybe you could take out the straw, Jayne, after all the girls get here."

Katie's mother nodded, and Mrs. Williams stroked Katie's cheek affectionately. "Thank you for inviting him, Katie," she said. "I know you didn't have to. He's really been excited about coming."

Katie flushed a little. "I'm glad he wanted to come. I hope he has fun."

"We match," Louis said again, smiling.

The doorbell rang again, and Katie answered it. Esther and her sisters were on the front porch. Esther's skinny legs were sticking out beneath a mass of white netting that shot out from her waist. Her light blond hair was rolled in tight curls all over her head.

Sharon was dressed in a long green shirt and tights, and she had a little green cap on her head. Susanna wore a ruffled blouse and had her pant legs tucked into Mrs. Gresham's high-heeled boots. She also had a black patch over one eye and a tinfoil hook taped to her right hand.

Louis screamed when he saw her. But Susanna just laughed and lifted up the patch to show him her eye.

"I'm Captain Hook," she said. "And Sharon's Peter Pan."

"And you're Tinker Bell, aren't you?" Katie asked Esther.

"Yeah. Are you Dorothy? I like the ruby slippers."

"Thanks." Katie smiled. "And I like your outfit. Where'd you get it?"

"It's Jillian's old ballerina tutu. She let me borrow it."

Jillian came as Little Bo Peep. She had on a frilly Sunday dress, and she carried a stuffed lamb under one arm. On her other arm, she carried her grandfather's cane. Louis asked her what the cane was, and she tossed her curly red head and said, "It's a shepherd's staff, of course."

Tracy came dressed like Snow White, wearing a white, puffed-sleeve blouse and a long blue skirt. Rising from the top of her cape was a white piece of paper that was supposed to be her stand-up collar. But Katie noticed that it didn't stand up long.

When Renee arrived, Katie caught her breath. Renee had on a long, lacy pink gown with a wide ribbon tied around her waist. When she walked into the living room,

Katie could see that she even had pink ballet slippers on her feet. Her hair was put up and topped with a rhinestone crown, and she carried a little hand fan.

"That dress is beautiful, Renee," said Jillian. "You're Cinderella, aren't you?"

"Yes," said Renee, with a smile.

"Did you get that dress just for this party?" Tracy asked.

Renee turned to Tracy and laughed. "Of course not. I wore this for the All-State Children's Orchestra auditions last year."

Tracy blushed.

"Tracy got a new blouse to wear for the party, didn't you, Tracy?" said Esther quickly.

Tracy nodded. "I was going to get it anyway, though."

"Who are you supposed to be?" Renee asked, peering at Tracy while she fanned herself lightly with her little fan.

"I'm Snow White," said Tracy, growing redder.

Renee chuckled and whispered to Jillian, "She looks more like Dopey, don't you think?"

It was then that Mrs. Crawford came into the room. She looked right at Tracy and said cheerfully, "You girls all look so pretty today! And Louis over there looks very handsome."

Louis laughed, and Renee looked at him.

"What's he doing here?" she asked Jillian.

"I don't know," Jillian said. "He's never come before."

"Katie and I play with Louis sometimes," said Esther, looking at neither Renee nor Katie.

The party began with games and prizes and then moved to the present-opening time. Katie liked this part the best. Mr. Crawford and Jeffers came to the doorway to watch her open her gifts.

As soon as Katie sat down, Renee quickly handed her a gift.

"Open mine first," she said.

Inside the small box was an evening gown for a doll, with shiny sequins all over the dress and a lot of netting underneath the skirt to make it stand out.

The other girls looked at Renee unhappily. Katie thanked her and reached for the next present.

Tracy gave her a coloring book and crayons.

"I haven't colored in a coloring book since first grade," whispered Renee to Jillian.

"Well, I like it," said Katie, looking at Tracy. "Thank you."

"Open my book next," said Louis. "Open my book. Read me a story?"

"All right, Louis," said Katie, laughing as she set aside a beautiful copy of *Little Women*.

"Now?" he asked, moving to sit next to her.

"Not right now," she said.

Jillian's present was a little pink hand mirror, brush, and comb set. It came with a matching pink tray to put everything on.

Katie opened Esther's gift last. There was a pencil holder, a set of water colors and brushes, and a large blotter made out of construction paper covered with plastic.

"I made the blotter and pencil holder myself," said Esther. "I hope you like them. The plastic is in case you spill the water colors on your blotter."

"Thanks, Esther. It'll be fun to use!"

"You know, homemade presents never look quite right," Renee whispered to Jillian.

Katie ignored Renee's comment and began opening the present from her mom and dad. It was a lush green velvet dress with cream lace and pearl buttons.

"That's pretty," said Renee, eyeing the dress as Katie pulled it from the box.

"And my mom even made it," answered Katie, smiling.

Renee didn't answer.

Jeffers gave Katie a heart-shaped locket. As Mrs. Crawford clasped the locket around Katie's neck, Mr. Crawford brought in a huge box, which he set in the middle of the living room floor.

Katie looked at her smiling parents, tore off the wrappings, and opened up the box.

"Oh! Oh!" she cried. "Daddy, help me get it out! Oh! You bought it after all! Oh, thank you, thank you!"

She jumped up and gave them both hugs. Mr. Crawford drew the present out of the box. It was the town house from the toy store. He had already assembled it.

The girls all breathed in admiration and scooted closer to see it. It had three floors, two balconies, and an elevator that moved up and down by pulling a cord. The living room had built-in bookshelves. The kitchen had cabinets full of food boxes and cans, and the dining room had sliding patio doors that opened onto a terrace.

"Is that ever neat," said Esther. "What a birthday present!"

"When can we play with it, Katie?" asked Renee, coming to sit next to her. "I could play with this house every day of the week."

"So could I," said Jillian.

"Let's play right now," said Katie. "I've got all my stuff upstairs—"

"No, we'll have to come over here one at a time," said Renee. "We can't play with this many people."

"It's time to eat now, so everybody come into the dining room for cake and ice cream," said Mrs. Crawford.

"All right! Yum, yum!" said Louis, jumping up.

The girls found their places at the table. Esther sat on one side of Katie, and Renee sat on the other. Louis ended up sitting at the opposite end of the table.

"You want to play on Monday?" Renee asked Katie as soon as they were seated.

Esther turned to her sister Sharon, as if she weren't listening.

"Sure," said Katie. "You want to play over here?"

Renee laughed. "You're the one with all the fancy stuff."

Mrs. Crawford came in and passed out the bowls of ice cream. Katie blew out her candles and cut the cake.

"So how is everything?" Mrs. Crawford asked later from the kitchen doorway. She glanced at Louis who was sitting at the end of the table, stabbing cake with his fork and chewing with his mouth open.

"This cake is very good," said Esther.

"Why, thank you, Esther."

"What kind of cake is this, Katie?" Renee asked. "Is it butterscotch or something? My favorite is German chocolate, with its special coconut frosting. I'll bet you've never had that, have you?"

"No," said Katie slowly.

"Hey, where were you yesterday?" Renee asked her. "Why didn't you come to the golf course to go sledding? Jillian came, and we had a great time!"

"It just didn't work out," mumbled Katie.

"You should've come, Katie," Renee continued. "The snow was really deep and slippery. It was cold out, though, because the sun had started setting by the time we got there. It never gets this cold in Indiana until January. I hope it's not like this all winter. I can't believe how much snow you have here."

"I build a snowman," said Louis, finishing his third piece of cake.

Renee ignored him and said to the others, "If we're going to have snow all winter, I hope we get lots of snow days. Jillian and I had so much fun yesterday."

"I played by myself," said Tracy, frowning.

"Me too," said Louis. "You play with me?" He looked at Tracy.

"Uh—well, I don't know," said Tracy.

"What about your friend Robbie?" Katie asked Louis. "Can't you have him over to play?"

"I dunno."

Sitting next to Katie, Renee fidgeted, her ears and cheeks growing red.

"Who's Robbie?" Esther asked Katie.

"He's one of Louis's friends at the Center," said Katie.

Renee stood up quickly and put her napkin on the table. "I have to go," she said. "I don't feel good."

"Oh, I'm sorry," said Mrs. Crawford. "I'll get your coat. Do you need a ride home?"

"No, I'll walk." She took her coat and ran out the front door.

All the girls sat looking at one another in surprise.

"Is Renee really sick, Mom?" Katie asked.

Mrs. Crawford paused before answering. "She didn't look too well."

Chapter Eleven

David and Mephibosheth

"Good morning, Katie," said Miss Carmichael as Katie entered the fifth grade girls' Sunday school classroom. "You look nice today! Is that a new dress?"

Katie smiled and glanced down at her soft, green velvet dress. "Yes, thank you. I got it for my birthday."

"That's right, you had a birthday this week," said Miss Carmichael.

The other girls were all sitting down. Katie noticed that they had turned around and looked at her when she came in.

Katie stayed at the door with Miss Carmichael because she couldn't decide where to sit. Renee and Jillian were seated in one row. Esther was sitting next to Tracy in the row directly in front of them. There was an empty chair next to Esther and an empty one next to Renee.

Esther smiled at Katie, took her Bible off the seat beside her, and put it under her chair. But Renee also motioned for Katie to come sit by her.

"I'm going to play with Katie's new town house tomorrow," said Renee to Jillian, as she watched Esther out of the corner of her eye.

Esther turned toward the front and began talking to Tracy.

Miss Carmichael closed the classroom door. "All right, I guess it's time to start. Katie, can you find a seat?"

Renee motioned to Katie again. Esther continued talking to Tracy.

So, with her heart skipping beats, Katie slipped into the seat beside Renee.

"Well," said Miss Carmichael cheerfully, "how was your week? I'm sure you all had fun playing in the snow on Friday. I missed not having you in art class, but I enjoyed my day off too."

Tracy raised her hand. "Did you build a snowman?"

Miss Carmichael laughed. "No, but I was outside. My big pine tree was all covered with snow, and so I went out and painted a picture of it. It was just lovely!"

"Wow!" breathed the girls in admiration.

"Can you bring your picture to art class this week so we can see it?" Katie asked.

Miss Carmichael smiled. "Certainly."

Renee turned to Jillian and said under her breath, "I wouldn't sit outside in the snow and freeze to death just to paint a picture."

"Tracy, why don't you come help me lead songs today?" Miss Carmichael asked. Happily, Tracy went to stand by Miss Carmichael in front of the other girls.

First they sang "Happy Birthday" to Katie, and she picked from the Birthday Box a bookmark with Psalm 23 written on it. Then all the girls stood up to sing "Whiter Than Snow" and "Heavenly Sunshine." Tracy held up the song sheets.

After the first song Jillian stopped singing in her pretty soprano voice to watch Tracy. She whispered scornfully to Renee, "Tracy has a squeaky voice, doesn't she?"

Renee agreed and whispered to Jillian that Tracy should have worn her Dopey collar to church. Renee and Jillian giggled quietly.

Katie squirmed in her seat because she could hear what they were saying. She hoped Esther couldn't hear. Esther might think that Katie agreed with Renee and Jillian about Tracy. Katie couldn't understand why Jillian was laughing at Tracy. After all, they had been best friends before Renee moved to town.

Soon the singing was over, and Miss Carmichael had them all sit down so she could tell the Bible lesson. Every week Miss Carmichael drew pictures on the chalkboard to illustrate the Bible story.

Miss Carmichael asked her class, "Who can tell me the most famous friends mentioned in the Bible?"

Everyone's hand went up. Miss Carmichael looked around the room. "All right, Esther. Who were they?"

"David and Jonathan," said Esther in her small voice.

"Good," said Miss Carmichael. She opened her Bible and turned some pages. "Girls, find I Samuel 18 in your Bibles. Verse 1 says: 'And it came to pass, when he had made an end of speaking unto Saul, that the soul of Jonathan was knit with the soul of David, and Jonathan loved him as his own soul.' "

Miss Carmichael went to the chalkboard and drew Jonathan and David. Jonathan was wearing a purple robe with a furry white collar; beneath the robe he had on a pink tunic. David just had on a brown tunic with a yellow sash. They both wore sandals with straps that laced up their legs.

Then Miss Carmichael drew Jonathan's giving his purple robe to David. "This shows that Jonathan loved David so much that he was willing to give up his right to be king of Israel because he knew that God wanted David to be king instead of him," explained Miss Carmichael. "I wonder how much you love your friends."

Katie looked at the back of Esther's light-blond head. She wondered what Esther was thinking.

Next Miss Carmichael drew Jonathan and David out in a green field. Jonathan and David were shaking hands. Jonathan had on his pink tunic and David had on Jonathan's purple robe. Miss Carmichael said they were making a covenant with each other.

Tracy raised her hand. "What's a covenant?"

Miss Carmichael smiled at her. "That's a good question, Tracy. Does anyone know?"

Renee tossed her head. "It's a vow or a promise."

"Very good," said Miss Carmichael. "David promised Jonathan that he would take care of Jonathan's family after he died. You see, whenever a new king came to the throne, he would often kill the rest of the old king's family so that no one would try to take the kingdom away from him. Because Jonathan and David were true friends, David promised Jonathan that he would take care of Jonathan's family for him instead of killing them."

Miss Carmichael looked at the girls in her classroom one by one, starting with the girls on the other side of the room. Then she looked at Tracy and at Jillian; she looked at Esther and then Katie. Finally, she looked at Renee.

"There is one particular lesson I want you to learn today," Miss Carmichael told the girls in a very serious voice. "I want you to learn what true friendship is. You cannot be someone's friend unless you are loyal. Loyalty is the cord that ties friends together. It doesn't matter how nice you are to their face or how much you like playing with them. What matters is if you are loyal. If you stick up for them."

Miss Carmichael went back to the board and drew a battlefield. There were lots of chariots and horses and men holding spears and shields. The picture filled up most of the chalkboard. In the next scene Miss Carmichael showed Jonathan and Saul lying dead on the ground.

"Because Saul and Jonathan were killed in battle, David was made king," said Miss Carmichael. "What do you think happened once David became king?"

"He got a crown," said Tracy.

Renee gave a laugh, and Esther turned around and glared at her. Katie squirmed in her chair again.

"Yes," said Miss Carmichael, "but there was something else. David began to look for Jonathan's family, who were hiding because they were afraid David would kill them. Does anyone know the name of Jonathan's son?"

Renee raised her hand. "Mephibosheth."

Miss Carmichael looked surprised. "Very good, Renee. Yes, his name was Mephibosheth. Do you know what was unusual about him?"

Renee sat very still.

"Do you know, Renee?" asked Miss Carmichael.

Renee crossed her arms and shook her head. Her mouth was set in a hard line.

Katie raised her hand. "He had broken legs or something."

"Even more sad than that. He was crippled—he couldn't walk without help. We would call him 'disabled' today." Miss Carmichael drew Mephibosheth on the chalkboard. His legs were crooked and bandaged, and he had crutches under his arms.

"It was very sad," continued Miss Carmichael. "When Mephibosheth's family was running to get out of the palace, his nurse dropped him, and his legs became crippled. Tell me, what do most people think of disabled people today?"

The class was silent.

"Someone tell me," said Miss Carmichael. "I think you know."

Esther raised her hand. "They're afraid of them, and they make fun of them."

"Yes," said Miss Carmichael. "Do you know why?"

Katie gulped and nodded. She remembered all the things her parents had said to her about Louis.

"Why, Katie?" asked Miss Carmichael.

"Because they think they're better than them."

"That's right. Now tell me how you think a king would act toward a disabled person. Aren't kings used to being more important than everyone else?"

The class nodded.

"Then it would be natural for David to be mean to Mephibosheth or even to kill him. But what did he do? It's here in II Samuel 9, verses 6 and 7." Miss Carmichael turned several pages in her Bible and read.

> Now when Mephibosheth, the son of Jonathan, the son of Saul, was come unto David, he fell on his face, and did

> reverence. And David said, Mephibosheth. And he answered, Behold thy servant!
>
> And David said unto him, Fear not: for I will surely shew thee kindness for Jonathan thy father's sake, and will restore thee all the land of Saul thy father; and thou shalt eat bread at my table continually.

Miss Carmichael looked up at her class. "What would you think of David if he had not been kind to Mephibosheth?"

"He wouldn't have been a very good friend," said Esther.

"No, he wouldn't have been good at all," agreed Miss Carmichael. "He would have been a liar because he had made a promise to Jonathan. But he didn't promise Mephibosheth anything, did he?"

The girls shook their heads.

"So do you think Mephibosheth expected David to take care of him?" Miss Carmichael asked.

The girls shook their heads again.

"You see," said Miss Carmichael, "Mephibosheth didn't expect it because David wasn't his friend. He probably also didn't expect it because he was handicapped. Have you ever noticed that disabled people don't expect much? Take Louis Williams, for example. Does Louis need much attention to make him happy?"

Katie shifted in her seat. She remembered pushing Louis in the school swing and reading to him at the Center. She thought of his smiles. She blushed as she also recalled yelling at Louis to do his Rumplestiltskin part correctly. She wondered if Esther were remembering that too.

Miss Carmichael continued, "Although Mephibosheth did not expect David to be kind to him, David was kind—because it was *right*. You girls know who your good friends are. You must decide to be a true and loyal friend to everyone—even to girls who aren't friendly—because it is the right thing to do."

The classroom was completely silent. Esther was looking straight ahead. Tracy was fidgeting with her dress. Jillian was biting her lip. And Renee was sitting stiffly, her green eyes fixed on the floor, her chin set firmly.

Katie took a long breath. She wanted to cry because she felt so guilty. Miss Carmichael prayed and let the girls out for the church service.

Katie couldn't listen during church. Instead, she looked up the passages that Miss Carmichael had read from I and II Samuel. She read them again for herself. She decided that after church she would find Louis and thank him again for the book he had given her for her birthday. That might make him happy.

After the church service had ended, Katie walked outside with Renee. Renee wanted to set up the best time for them to play with Katie's town house the following day.

As they walked down the sidewalk, Katie spotted Louis swinging on the homemade tire swing behind the church. The tire hung from an oak branch by a thick chain. Louis was spinning around in circles, his tongue hanging from his mouth.

Barry Logan and Joel Kirby were standing a short distance away in snow that was up to their ankles, packing snowballs.

The snow was melting all around the parking lot, making wet puddles in the low parts of the pavement. The old snow, crispy and sharp-edged, seemed to pull away from the sidewalks. Patches of brown grass pricked through the crusts of ice.

Katie left Renee on the sidewalk and tiptoed through the snow over to the tire swing.

"Hi, Ka-tie!" said Louis as his spins slowed down.

"Hi, Louis," she answered. She stopped in front of the tire swing. "Louis, I starting reading your book last night. I like it a lot!"

"My book?" He looked at her with his mouth open.

"The book you gave me for my birthday."

"Oh, yeah. I forgot." Louis grinned. "Fun party. Yum, yum! Happy Birthday!"

Katie laughed. "Thanks for coming, Louis. And thanks for the book."

"You let the retard come to your birthday party?" Barry shouted to her.

"Hey, retard!" shouted Joel. "Did you go to a girls' party?"

Louis looked at Joel blankly.

"The retard can't remember if he went or not," jeered Barry. "Hey, retard, did you eat cake and ice cream?"

"Did you play 'Pin-the-tail-on-the-donkey'?"

Barry and Joel began to laugh hysterically.

Katie clenched her fists and shouted angrily, "Why don't you two pick on someone else? You're so nasty to Louis!"

"Why don't you pick on someone else?" mimicked Joel.

"You're as stupid as Louis if you invited him to your party," said Barry.

"I am not stupid!" shouted Katie hotly.

Louis glared at the boys. "You're stupid!" he yelled.

Barry picked up a hard ice ball. "If you're so smart, catch this!" he said as he tossed it at Louis.

The snowball splintered against the tire, spraying snow into Louis's face.

"Leave Louis alone!" Katie threatened, grabbing a handful of snow and throwing it back.

The boys laughed as the unpacked snow floated to the ground.

"You want a snowball fight?" Joel called. "Catch this!" He whipped a hard ice ball at Katie.

It smashed into her chest, shooting a pang through her whole body.

"Stop it! That hurt!" screamed Katie.

Another snowball sailed into her face. It stung when it hit her, as though she had just been slapped. Her face felt hot and tingly. She sputtered and tried to wipe the snow out of her eyes and hair. A cold headache began throbbing behind her eyes.

She turned around, but two more snowballs flew into her back and legs. The ice began melting against her skin, and the wind licked at her wet face. Her cheeks stung as she brushed away hot tears.

She heard the chain on the tire swing clank, and then she heard Barry and Joel screaming, and then the shouts of other children who were running past her.

She turned around and squinted through her tears.

Louis was rolling on the ground with Barry and Joel, pushing their faces into the snow, wildly pouncing on them, and yelling like an Indian. The boys were clawing and kicking and gasping for air. But Louis was bigger and heavier than both of them.

Adults and children were coming from all over the parking lot. Mr. Crawford was the first to reach Louis. He climbed over the boys' legs and grabbed Louis's arms. Louis was wild with anger, swinging his arms and feet. Saliva ran down his chin. Mr. Crawford pulled him off the boys and held his arms tightly.

Mrs. Williams came running up with Mrs. Crawford. "Louis!" she cried. "What are you doing?"

Katie's mom came over to her and gently wiped her face. "What happened to you?" She dabbed at Katie's eyes and brushed the snow off her coat and dress.

Barry and Joel got to their feet. They were sweaty and dirty, and they choked as they tried to breathe.

"What happened here?" said Mr. Crawford sternly. "Katie, what happened?"

Katie began to cry.

"L-Louis at-tacked us," Barry panted.

"Louis!" said Mrs. Williams.

"They started throwing snowballs at Katie first," someone said.

"And then Louis got out of the swing and jumped on them!" someone else exclaimed.

Louis was panting heavily, staring at the ground, silent.

"Louis, is this true?" asked Mrs. Williams.

Tears came into his eyes also, and he hung his head. "Th-they were l-laughing, and—and th-they h-hurt K-kat-ie."

Katie walked to Louis and gave his hand a squeeze. "Thank you, Louis, for helping me," she whispered, and then she began to cry again. "They were calling him names," she shouted angrily to the group. "They were calling him a retard." She glared at Barry and Joel.

Mrs. Crawford pulled Katie into her arms. “Are you sure you’re all right, honey?”

Katie gave a loud sniffle.

“Daddy will handle this,” continued her mother quietly. “Come inside with me and we’ll get you cleaned up.” She guided Katie away from the group of children.

They stepped through the patchy snow toward the sidewalk that led to the back church door. Even through her tears, Katie could see Renee still standing there on the sidewalk, watching silently.

Chapter Twelve

Renee's Secret

The snow was nearly gone by Friday. Katie hoped it would snow again before Thanksgiving because her class chorus was singing "Over the River and Through the Woods" at the Thanksgiving program.

Katie loved rehearsing for the fifth grade Pilgrim play. Her role was the best girls' part because it had the most lines. Renee only played a walk-on Indian squaw who carried an arm load of cornstalks. Renee said that walk-on parts were better than speaking parts because you didn't get nervous. But she said she wouldn't be nervous about her violin solo either, because she was playing "Come, Ye Thankful People, Come," and it was only an easy hymn. Jillian was singing a solo again this year, "We Gather Together"; so she and Renee had become constant companions.

After practice on Friday, Miss Lauren asked all the children with big parts to stay because Barry was having trouble with his lines. Katie told her friends that whoever wanted to come to her house should wait for her by the school's front doors. She thought that would be the best way to decide who should come over to play with the town house. Each of the girls had been over once already that week, and they all wanted to come over again.

"Let's start again at Barry's line," said Miss Lauren, brushing a strand of golden hair out of her face. "Now, Barry, think of your lines. You are Squanto. He's a friendly Indian, not a warrior. Go back and enter through that door on your right."

Barry re-entered. "How," he mumbled unenthusiastically. "I come to bring squash for white man's feast."

Katie sighed and glanced around the stage. She wondered where her parents would sit during the program. Renee's parents would probably sit in front of the orchestra, and so she knew her parents wouldn't sit with them. Mr. Crawford hated sitting near the orchestra because they squeaked all the way through their songs.

"I want—I want—" said Barry.

"I want to keep—" Miss Lauren helped.

"I want to keep peace—"

"—with white man—" Miss Lauren said.

"I want to keep peace with white man—for many moons," said Barry.

"All right," said Miss Lauren, looking tired. "The rest of you may go home. I guess there's no need for you to wait while we go over Squanto's lines. Barry, you stay so we can work on this."

Katie ran down the stage steps and gathered up her things. She hurried through the halls toward the front doors. As she neared the final corner, she could hear the girls talking.

"Miss Lauren showed the program to me because my name is on it," Renee was saying.

"Are any of our names on it?" Tracy asked.

"Only Jillian's and mine," said Renee, "because we're soloists and you're not."

Jillian giggled.

"Katie's name isn't on it?" asked Esther.

"Why should it be?" said Renee scornfully.

Katie stopped by the corner and stood close to the wall so they couldn't see her. She felt a lump in her throat.

"She has the biggest girls' part in the Pilgrim play," said Esther.

"So? We all have parts. The program just says that the play is done by the fifth grade class."

"I just thought they'd put her name on it," said Esther quietly, " 'cause she's Priscilla Alden and everything."

"Barry's a terrible Squanto," said Jillian. "He doesn't even know his lines."

"He sure looks mean with those black and blue marks all over his face," said Tracy.

"Louis should be locked up for doing that to him," said Renee. "He acted like an animal on Sunday."

Anger leaped into Katie's heart. She wanted to run out into the hall and hit Renee.

"Louis is not an animal!" exclaimed Esther. "He's a person, just like us."

"He may be like you, but he's not like me!" Renee replied hotly.

"He's nicer than you, that's for sure! You just stood there while Barry and Joel were hitting Katie with ice balls!" Esther's voice rose to a high squeak. "At least Louis tried to help Katie when you wouldn't!"

There was an awkward silence in the hallway. Katie felt frozen to her spot. The other girls seemed afraid to move also.

Finally Renee said in a harsh voice, "Katie asked for it because she invited Louis to her birthday party. Nobody with brains has a retard to her birthday party."

"Louis didn't hurt anything," said Esther. "We had a lot of fun."

"That town house was the best part of the party," said Tracy cautiously.

"I didn't think it was all that great," Renee argued. "It's only made out of plastic and paper. And the elevator doesn't look strong enough to hold up a doll."

"Oh, that's too bad," said Tracy. "The elevator's the best part."

Katie's heart was beating faster. She strained to hear every word.

"I like it—" began Esther.

"You would say that," Renee interrupted. "You don't even have a doll house." Then she continued to the others, "Katie'll probably break it, you know. She can be so clumsy."

"She jumped into my rope at recess today and messed me all up," said Jillian. "I had to quit at thirty-two."

"Jillian and I got sixty-three yesterday," said Renee.

Tears squeezed into Katie's eyes. How could they talk about her like that?

Just then Barry Logan opened the door at the other end of the hall. Even from down the hall Katie could see a purplish ring around his eyes and nose. He glared at her.

Katie stepped out into the hallway and walked away from him, toward the girls. Renee whispered "Shh!" to the others and stood there smiling.

With her eyes on the linoleum floor, Katie blinked back tears and walked straight to the front doors and pushed them open. Quickly she crossed the school yard and headed for Maple Lane.

"Hey, I thought you wanted us to wait for you," called Renee behind her.

Katie gave a little sob and walked faster. The winter wind dried the tears around her eyes and made her face feel tight.

"Katie—" called Esther, coming after her. "Wait up!"

She pretended not to hear. She wanted to get away from all of them, even Esther. She wanted to go to some place quiet and sit on her mom's lap and feel loved.

She wouldn't go home alone. She would go to the Center to see her mom. Katie turned and ran across the playground toward Chestnut Street instead. Esther called again, but Katie ran faster. She ran all the way to Birch Street before she slowed down. She couldn't wait to get to the Center to see her mom. She would play with Louis and Robbie today instead of the girls. Louis and Robbie never said anything bad about her.

The Center looked warm and comforting as it stood on Birch Street, guarded by the little orange school bus in the street. Katie made sure her eyes were dry before she opened the Center's front door and went in.

Robbie spotted her first. "Ka-tie!" He came up and gave her legs a hug.

Katie led him into the playroom and set down her book bag. Louis wasn't in the room. Mrs. Crawford was straightening some shelves nearby.

"I thought you were playing with your town house after school today, honey," said Mrs. Crawford with a smile.

The tears returned to Katie's eyes. She ran to her mother and wrapped her arms around her mom's waist.

"What is it? What happened?" Mrs. Crawford held her close and stroked her hair.

Katie began to sob.

Mrs. Crawford said nothing for a couple of minutes. Then she led her to the rocking chair and pulled her onto her lap. "Now tell Mom what happened today to make my girl cry like this."

"Th-they were t-talking about m-me," she stammered.

"Who was?"

"R-renee—"

Mrs. Crawford's face hardened. Her brown eyes looked angry. "Are you sure?" She looked directly into Katie's eyes.

"Y-yes—and the others were, t-too. I heard all of them."

"Where were you?"

Katie took a deep breath and tried to stop sniffling. "I had to stay late for practice, and I told them to wait for me at the door, and when I was coming to the door, they were all there talking, and I heard them around the corner."

Mrs. Crawford smoothed Katie's hair and wiped her tears away. "Eavesdropping is never good, honey."

"I didn't mean to listen. But I heard my name—"

"I know, I know."

Katie gave another sniff. "Renee was making fun of my town house and of my being Priscilla in the play. And then she said I was clumsy."

Mrs. Crawford shook her head. "She's just jealous, honey. People can get very nasty when they're jealous of someone. You see, Renee is very insecure. That means that she's unhappy with herself because she doesn't know for sure how much her family and friends love her. It's like being really hungry for food, except that Renee is hungry for attention. She feels that she has to be good at everything so that people will like her."

"But she is good at everything," said Katie.

"No, it just seems like that. Why do you think she criticized your part in the play?"

"I don't know."

"Because she knows that you're a better actress than she is. That's why you got the biggest part. Now it doesn't always work that way, but a lot of times it does."

"Oh," said Katie, feeling better. "Does that mean she still likes me or not?"

"Well, I don't know how much she likes you. But I don't think that anyone who talks behind your back is really your friend."

"But they all talked."

"All of them?" said Mrs. Crawford. "Was Esther there? What did she say?"

Katie thought. "I guess you're right. Esther didn't say anything bad. And neither did Tracy."

"There now," Mrs. Crawford said. "What does that tell you? Now why don't you go play with Robbie and get your mind off the whole thing. Louis is out with Mrs. Williams, but they should be back soon."

"That was the other thing she said," Katie continued. "She was mad at Louis because he beat up Barry and Joel, and she said I asked for it because I invited a retard to my party."

Mrs. Crawford's eyes grew dark again.

Katie heard a shuffle in the hallway and saw that Mrs. Williams and Louis were taking off their coats.

After Mrs. Williams heard what had happened, she gave Katie a comforting smile. "I'm sorry the girls were so unkind to you, Katie."

Katie smiled weakly in return. "I'm sorry they were mean to Louis too."

Mrs. Williams turned to Louis. His cheeks were rosy from being outside. His squinty blue eyes looked up at his mother, and his mouth hung open as he watched her. Mrs. Williams brushed the blond hair off his forehead and stroked his face.

"Louis is very happy and fortunate to have you for a friend, Katie."

Katie got off Mrs. Crawford's lap and took Louis's hand. They walked over to Robbie and sat down on the floor with him. "Let's read a story, okay?" Katie said. Mrs. Crawford smiled at her and rose to talk with Mrs. Williams.

Katie picked up a book of fairy tales. "What should I read?" she asked them.

"A story," said Louis.

"How 'bout a winter story, since it's so cold today?" Katie asked.

Robbie nodded.

Katie opened to the table of contents and read down the list of titles. "Here's one. My mom read this to me a long time ago."

Katie turned to the story and showed them a watercolor picture of a little girl in rags, crouched next to a brick building. She held several long wooden matches in her hand. The boys snuggled close to look.

"'The Little Match Girl' by Hans Christian Andersen," began Katie. "'It was late on a bitterly cold, snowy New Year's Eve. A poor little girl was wandering in the dark, cold streets; she was bareheaded and barefooted,'" Katie read. "That means she didn't have any shoes," she added.

"I have shoes," said Louis.

"Me too," said Robbie, holding out his feet for them to see.

Katie smiled and continued, " 'She carried a quantity of matches in her old apron and held a packet of them in her hand. No one had bought any from her during all the long day. . . .' "

The boys sat wide-eyed as Katie read the sad tale of the little match girl who sat down next to a building and lit the matches that she was supposed to sell. She was very, very cold. With every lit match, she pretended to see a warm room. But then the match would go out, and she would be cold and lonely again.

Katie continued reading earnestly, " 'She struck a new one; it burned, it blazed up, and where the light fell upon the wall against which she lay . . . she could see right through it into the room inside. There was a table, spread with a snowy cloth and pretty china—' "

"I like snow," said Louis. "I build snowman."

"Me too," Katie answered, "but this snow is just describing the tablecloth where the people eat."

"I like to eat!" exclaimed Louis.

"Want to hear what kind of food there was?" Katie asked. Louis nodded, and so Katie continued: " 'A roast goose stuffed with apples and prunes was steaming on the table. And what was even better, the goose hopped from the dish, with the carving knife and fork sticking in his back, and it waddled across the floor.' "

"The goose was playing tricks," Katie explained. "I'll bet that made the little girl even hungrier to see that goose running around when she wanted to eat it so badly."

"Don't play with your food," said Louis seriously.

Katie giggled. "Do you play with your food, Louis?"

"Yep," said Louis.

"Can I finish the story now?" Katie asked him.

"Yep."

"'And then the match went out and there was nothing to be seen but the thick black wall.' " Katie felt sad for the little girl sitting out in the snow.

She read faster. " 'Now she struck another match against the wall, and this time it was her grandmother who appeared in the circle of flame. She saw her quite clearly and distinctly, looking so gentle and happy. "Grandmother!" cried the little creature. "Oh, do take me with you! I know you will vanish when the match goes out!" She hastily struck a whole bundle of matches because she did so want to keep her grandmother with her. The light of the matches made it as bright as day. . . . Grandmother had never before looked so big or so beautiful. She lifted the little girl up in her arms, and they soared in a halo of light and joy, far, far above the earth, where there was no more cold, no hunger, no pain, for they were with God.' "

Katie paused before she read the next sentence. "'In the cold morning light, the poor little girl sat there, in the corner between the houses, with rosy cheeks and a smile on her face—dead.' "

Katie took a deep breath and gave a quiet sniff. She felt as though she had lost a friend.

"What happened?" Louis asked.

"She died because she was so cold and hungry. No one loved her. No one cared if she lived or not. She had only one friend, and that was her grandma." Katie solemnly closed the book.

Louis thought for a minute. "I have two friends."

Katie smiled. "Who are they?"

"Ka-tie and R-r-robbie."

"What about Esther?"

"Oh, yeah. I forgot. I like girls."

"Thank you, Louis. I like you too."

Katie felt a gust of cold air enter the room as the Center's front door creaked open. Mrs. Williams left to see who it was.

"Robbie, your sister's here to get you," she called. "Come get dressed to leave."

Katie got up to put the book away. Robbie slowly walked into the hallway.

"Hurry up, Robbie," said an impatient voice from the doorway. "Dad's got the car running."

Katie could hear the thump of Robbie's boots being pulled on, and then the swishing of his ski jacket.

"No, Robbie, that's the wrong sleeve," said the voice again. "No, that's the hood! Can't you do anything right?"

The voice sounded strangely familiar, and Katie walked to the doorway to see the sister who was being so mean to Robbie.

Then she realized that it was Renee standing in the hallway with Robbie, thrusting his short little arms into the padded sleeves and dropping the mittens on the floor.

"Renee—!" said Katie.

Renee stared at her with a white, horrified face. Then she grabbed Robbie's arm and dragged him out the door.

Chapter Thirteen

Cookies and Milk

" 'O, come, let us sing unto the Lord: let us make a joyful noise to the rock of our salvation,' " read Mr. Crawford. " 'Let us come before his presence with thanksgiving, and make a joyful noise unto him with psalms.' "

Mr. Crawford closed his Bible and set it on the dining room table. He put his arm around Mrs. Crawford, pulled her toward him, and gave her a kiss. "I'm thankful for Mom because she's a wonderful wife and mother—"

"Oh, Alan," said Mrs. Crawford, smiling.

"And I'm thankful for our home, shop, and church, and for you kids. What about the rest of you?"

"I'm very grateful for all of you too," said Mrs. Crawford. "You kids make us so proud. I'm also thankful for the children at the Center."

Katie took a deep breath. "I'm glad the Thanksgiving program went okay last night, and that Barry remembered most of his lines." She paused and blushed slightly. "I guess I'm most thankful for my family and friends—especially Esther and Louis."

Mrs. Crawford smiled.

Jeffers said quickly, "I'm glad we won our last football game and that Mom is such a good cook. When can we eat? I'm hungry!"

Everyone laughed and then took the hands of those beside them while Mr. Crawford asked the blessing on the food.

"You know," Mrs. Crawford said during the meal, "I've got to bake and freeze four dozen Christmas cutout cookies today for the Center's Christmas pageant. And I've got to make angel costumes for the children too! So—I need a few volunteers to help me with all those cookies."

"All right!" exclaimed Katie. "I'll help!"

"Me too, during the commercials," chimed in Jeffers.

Mrs. Crawford shook her head at him. "Jeffers, you can't run back and forth during the whole football game."

"Then I'll just help you eat them."

"That's what I thought you were after," she said.

Jeffers grinned at her.

"I've already got the dough made and chilled, Katie. You want to start right after dinner?"

"Yeah! That'll be fun."

"Now, Katie," her mother continued, "once I've got the cookies all baked, I'll have to start sewing. Maybe you'd like to invite a friend over to help you decorate them. It's going to take all day."

Katie looked at the table. "You think Esther would want to come? She hasn't been over here for a long time."

"Yes, I think so," said Mrs. Crawford, smiling. "Why don't you go call her when we're finished eating?"

After Katie helped her mom with the dishes, she dialed Esther's number. Her heart was pounding. What if she said she wouldn't come? Katie didn't know what she would say if Esther answered the phone first.

But Esther's mother answered.

"Mrs. Gresham . . . this is Katie. Do you think it would be okay if Esther came over today? We're going to cut out Christmas cookies for the Center's Christmas pageant." Katie paused for a second, breathing nervously. "Can she come right over? . . . Okay. Thanks. . . . Bye-bye."

Mrs. Crawford had already begun rolling out the dough when Esther arrived, and Katie was cutting out shapes with the cookie cutters. There were angels, donkeys, stars, bells, camels, wreaths, and trees. And, of course, there were lots of gingerbread men. Katie and Esther snitched as much dough as they could without Mrs. Crawford's scolding them. By the time they were finished cutting out cookie shapes, the first batches had already cooled and were ready to be iced.

Mrs. Crawford made white frosting and poured some into four small bowls. She let Katie and Esther color the frosting.

"Now don't put too much food coloring into those," she said to them. "Two drops is enough. Otherwise the color gets too dark."

"We know what we're doing," said Katie, giving the red food coloring bottle a hard squeeze.

Red liquid squirted all over the white frosting in one small bowl.

"I think you've got too much," Esther said. "Let's pour some out."

"It'll be fine. Wait 'til I stir it up."

Esther watched as Katie stirred.

"It's shocking pink," said Esther quietly.

Mrs. Crawford came over and had a look. "Now do you believe me?"

Esther laughed. "Who's doing the rest of the coloring now?"

"We will," said Katie promptly. "I'll do the green. You do the yellow and blue. But only put in two drops."

Esther giggled.

Mrs. Crawford left them to their decorating. Soon the frosting was all colored and the girls were busy putting yellow icing on the stars and green on the trees. They had red-hots and candy sprinkles and colored sugar crystals to put on the cookies too.

Katie poured them two tall, cold glasses of milk. Then they each ate a cookie and drank their milk.

"This is the most fun I've had in a long time," said Katie.

Esther looked at her steadily. "Even more fun than playing with Renee?"

Katie squirmed a little. "Yeah."

Esther put down her glass. "Do you like Renee more than me?"

"N-no. She hasn't been nice to me at all lately."

Esther finished her cookie and reached for a bell-shaped one. She spread blue icing on it and then sprinkled candies over the top. "Renee isn't nice to anyone."

"Sometimes she is."

"Only when she wants something."

Katie remembered the conversation she'd heard after the program practice. She could remember every sentence Renee had said. Katie sighed. "Yeah, I guess you're right. Look at all the things she said about me and my town house."

Esther stared at the table. "You heard, huh?"

Katie nodded.

"So she isn't your best friend anymore?" Esther watched Katie out of the corner of her eye.

"Well," Katie said, blushing, "she never really was my *best* friend. I mean—well, you and I have been best friends for a long time. . . ."

Esther smiled and put the bell with the other finished cookies. "Good," she said. "I like being your best friend, and I like it when you're mine."

Katie smiled too. "Esther," she said slowly, "I'm sorry I didn't play and talk to you more the whole time I was being Renee's friend. I guess I wasn't very nice."

"That's okay. I wasn't nice either." Esther blushed too and continued, "I didn't mean it when I said I never wanted to play with you again for the rest of my life. I'd rather play with you than anybody else."

Katie smiled broadly. "Me too."

The girls each took another cookie. Katie bit happily into the star she had chosen.

"Working hard, I see," said Mrs. Crawford, coming back into the kitchen.

"Yep," said Katie. She pointed to the white material draped over Mrs. Crawford's arm. "What's that?"

"Old sheets for the angel costumes. Can you believe Louis is going to be an angel?"

The girls giggled.

"He's going to be a pretty big one," said Esther.

"He and Robbie are singing 'Away in a Manger' at the Christmas pageant," Mrs. Crawford explained. "It's going to be so cute. We wanted Louis to sing with one of the children his age, but Robbie wouldn't sing with anyone else, and Louis wouldn't either."

"Who's Robbie?" asked Esther.

"You know, Louis's little friend at the Center," said Katie. "He's really latched on to Louis."

"Oh, yeah. You said something about him at your birthday party."

Mrs. Crawford went back to sewing. Both girls decorated a few more cookies in silence. Katie was thinking about how Renee had suddenly left her birthday party. She remembered the horrified look on Renee's face when they'd met later on at the Center.

"I guess Renee acts the way she does because she's so insecure," said Katie.

"What's that mean?" asked Esther.

"It means that she doesn't think people really like her."

"It's hard to like someone who's always making fun of you," said Esther.

"Yeah, I know. But Mom says she's like that because she's afraid people will find out about Rob—" Katie's eyes grew wide, and she clapped her hand over her mouth.

Esther looked confused. "Robbie? What does Renee have to do with him?"

Katie sighed. Mrs. Crawford had suggested that Katie not say anything about Renee's secret.

"It's just—well—I didn't mean to say anything," Katie stammered.

"Does Renee know Robbie?" Esther asked, sounding interested.

"Y-yes," Katie said.

"But she hates disabled kids," said Esther. "She hates Louis."

"Yeah, I know."

"Then how does she know Robbie? Why is she so mean to Louis if she likes disabled kids?"

"She doesn't like them. That's why she's mean to Louis." Katie paused and then said slowly, "You see, Robbie is Renee's brother."

Esther's mouth dropped open. "Renee has a disabled brother? She's the smartest girl in school! How come we never even knew she had a brother?"

"I guess he was still living in Indiana with his grandma until the Center opened up. They didn't want him to go to school where Renee went because she would be embarrassed. They didn't want anyone else to know about him."

"Really?"

"That's what Mr. St. Vincent told my mom."

They nibbled a little more on their cookies.

"It's too bad they act that way," said Esther.

"I know. Mom says that's why Robbie is so quiet. He's afraid of people."

"Don't his parents love him?" Esther sounded amazed.

Katie shrugged. "I don't know. Mom says that they don't seem to care about seeing him in the Christmas pageant."

Chapter Fourteen

The Christmas Pageant

"Don't our cookies look nice?" Katie said, beaming as she stepped back from the long reception table in the Center's playroom.

Esther finished arranging the stars, bells, and camels on another plate and stood beside her. "Yeah! The different colored frostings make them pretty, don't they?"

Katie nodded. "And the sprinkles. You don't think the red frosting is too bright, do you?"

She and Esther looked at the shocking-pink stockings on the plates.

Esther giggled. "Yeah, but they look nice, anyway."

Katie wandered along the table, inspecting the platters of desserts to be served after the Christmas pageant. Her mouth began to water. There were platters of fudge, frosted pretzels, and peanut brittle; and there were mounds of fluffy pink divinity and chocolate-covered peanut clusters. Peppermints stuck out of chocolate-frosted cupcakes. Cookies held chocolate kisses. Little chocolate brownies had green holly leaves frosted on them, with red-hots for berries. And there was one whole plate of candy canes with stripes of all colors.

Esther leaned over the table and whispered to Katie. "Think anybody would mind?"

"Naw!" said Katie, laughing, as she snatched a candy cane and two frosted pretzels. Esther took a big piece of fudge and carefully rearranged the other pieces on the plate.

"Umm!" they chorused as they munched.

Mrs. Crawford entered the room with a large glass bowl filled with red punch. She slowly set it down at the end of the table. "Is everything okay?" she asked with a slight smile.

Katie and Esther laughed, their mouths full. "Yep."

"The food looks very nice, girls. Thanks for helping me. Now, do you think you two could plug the tree in before Daddy brings the bus load of kids?"

"Sure," said Esther walking over to the blue spruce standing in front of the playroom windows.

"When's Louis getting here?" Katie asked.

"Any time," answered her mother. "Mrs. Williams said she'd be here early."

Katie went to stand beside Esther in front of the Christmas tree. It had tiny, blinking white lights and silver tinsel draped over the boughs. Everyone at the Center had made an ornament for it—even Katie. Louis had covered his with glue and multicolored glitter and hung it on the biggest branch in front. Robbie's and Katie's hung nearby.

Christmas lights and evergreen garlands were strung around the room, and big red bows hung at the tops of the windows.

"Katie," said Mrs. Crawford, "why don't you go over to the other room so when the children come, you and Esther can start helping them on with their costumes."

"Okay," said Katie. She and Esther took one last look at the tree and headed for the other room. Just then, the front door swung open, and the cold night air rushed in—along with Louis, Robbie, and Mrs. Williams.

"Hi, Ka-tie! Hi, Es-ther!" said Louis, dragging Robbie by the hand.

"Hi, Louis," said the girls.

"Merry Christ-mas," said Louis.

"Thank you. Merry Christmas to you too!" said Esther.

Mrs. Williams closed the door and took off her coat. She began to unwrap the scarves from Louis's and Robbie's necks. Katie and Esther helped with the mittens and zippers.

"Cook-ies!" exclaimed Louis as he looked past Katie at the table of food. "Yum! Yum!"

"Not now, Louis," said Katie. "You have to say your lines and sing your song in the pageant first. Then we'll eat."

"I want cookies."

But Katie and Esther guided the boys into the other room and began putting their costumes on them. There was a pile of neatly folded, white sheet-robes. Louis's costume was the largest.

Katie shook out the creases and stood on her tiptoes to get it over Louis's head. He wriggled as he put his arms into the sleeves. Esther found the smallest angel costume and put it on Robbie, who stood quietly without squirming. The wire halos, spray-painted gold, were ready to be put on the boys' heads.

"Do you know your lines, Louis?" Katie asked.

"Yep," said Louis. "When do I eat cookies?"

"After the pageant," she answered. "Do you remember where you sing your song?" Katie climbed up onto the simple plywood platform that her father had made. It stood at the end of the adults' classroom. Partitions had been set up on either side of the platform so there would be a "backstage" for the children when they didn't have a part to do.

"You will stand right here," said Katie. "And that light up there will be on you. Understand?"

But Louis was watching the children coming in the front door. Mr. Crawford and Jeffers had picked them all up in the little orange school bus. Their coats were taken off, and Mrs. Williams herded them into the room.

Mrs. Crawford began pulling different-colored costumes over the heads of the shepherds and wise men and tying sashes around their waists. She put scarves on the heads of all the shepherds.

"Who's going to be Mary and Joseph?" Katie asked, coming up to her.

"Krissy is Mary. And Billy is Joseph," said Mrs. Crawford as she worked. "Billy's standing over there in the blue costume."

Katie looked across the room at a thin, brown-haired boy. He stood straight and silent, watching the others around him as he held his staff. Katie saw only one arm hanging from his blue sleeves. She examined him more closely to see if there were another arm hidden somewhere in the folds of his mantle. It was so strange to see a boy with only one arm. Billy suddenly looked toward her, and Katie glanced away, embarrassed. She wondered how it felt to have only one arm.

"Come here please, Krissy," Mrs. Crawford called above the noise.

Krissy was wiping her nose and mouth on her sleeve.

"Now none of that," said Mrs. Crawford gently as she pulled Krissy into her arms and slipped a pink sheet-dress over her head. "I want you to be a lady up there. Remember, you have the very best part."

Krissy smiled.

"I have the bester part, too," said Louis, coming up.

"That's right," said Mrs. Crawford. "You're all important."

"All right," Mrs. Williams called out above the noise, "time for everyone to go behind the partitions. The parents are coming in."

Mrs. Williams took her place at the piano and began playing Christmas carols. Katie and Esther took the children backstage so the parents wouldn't see them.

"Where's Renee and her parents?" whispered Esther to Katie.

"I don't know," said Katie, looking around. "I haven't seen them." She secretly hoped Renee wouldn't come. She didn't want to see her. Katie hadn't talked to Renee since the day she overheard her gossiping.

"I wonder if they're going to come see Robbie."

Katie shrugged, but she was watching the Center's front door.

Louis peeked through the cracks between the partitions. "Mommy's playin' piano," said Louis.

Katie found her dad and Jeffers sitting toward the front. "There's my dad and Jeffers."

"There's my mom and dad," said Esther from her spot near a crack between the walls. "And my brothers and sisters."

Robbie put one eye up against the crack and looked around. The St. Vincents were not there. But Katie and

Esther watched other parents coming in. Katie heard them greet one another and talk about their children's parts in the program.

"Your momma come?" Louis asked Robbie.

But Robbie didn't answer. He just quietly looked around.

Katie felt hollow inside—hollow for him. She felt guilty for having wished that Renee and her parents wouldn't come to the pageant when Robbie needed them to come. Katie smoothed down Robbie's hair around the edge of his halo. Then she bent down and impulsively gave him a hug.

Soon Mrs. Williams stopped playing, and Mrs. Crawford walked to the front of the platform. "We're so happy to have you all here tonight," she said. "The children are so excited that they can hardly stand waiting. I think you'll be pleased and proud to see what they have prepared for us tonight. Pastor Gresham, would you please open this program with a word of prayer?"

When the prayer was over, the lights went out. There were two spotlights near the front. One light shone on the stable scene, and the other shone where the angel chorus would come out and sing. There were also three microphones, one at each light and one for the narrator.

A teen-age boy in a wheelchair, whose legs were thin and motionless, wheeled himself slowly out into the main spotlight. He put the brake on his chair and paused a moment as he looked out on the crowd.

Katie watched him closely.

When he began, a silence came over the audience. He spoke in a strong voice, as if the words were very important to him: " 'And it came to pass in those days, that there went out a decree from Caesar Augustus, that all the world should be taxed. . . .' "

The front door of the Center creaked open. Katie peeked through the crack to see.

"Look, Robbie," Esther whispered. A very tall man and a lady crept silently into the room and sat down in the last row. Renee was with them.

Katie's heart seemed to lift and sink at the same time.

Robbie smiled. "There's Mommy and Daddy!" he said. "And Rrrnay."

The other spotlight came up on the stable scene. Mary and Joseph were walking along the front of the stage. Joseph gave an imaginary knock at the inn's door.

The boy in the wheelchair answered the door. "Yes?"

Billy swallowed, looking nervous, and said, "My name is Joseph, and this is my wife Mary. We have journeyed all the way from Nazareth. We are very tired. Is there a room in your inn that we could stay in tonight?"

"I'm sorry," said the innkeeper. "All my rooms are full."

"But, please, can we stay somewhere?"

"Well, I have a stable out back. You may stay there if you like."

Mary and Joseph went to the stable and sat down on the floor. The light dimmed, and Krissy pulled a doll from underneath the manger and set it inside.

Then the boy in the wheelchair turned back to the audience and said, " 'And she brought forth her firstborn son, and wrapped him in swaddling clothes, and laid him in the manger; because there was no room for them in the inn.' "

That was the signal for the angel chorus to file out onto the stage. The children were going to recite the next seven verses of the Christmas story.

Louis recited verse 12. "And this shall be a sign to ye; Ye shall find the baby wrapped in saddle clothes, lying in a hanger."

The audience began to laugh. Louis grinned at them and gave a deep bow. They laughed again. Katie and Esther giggled behind the partitions.

When the Bible passage about the angels was finished, Mrs. Williams played the introduction to "Angels We Have Heard on High." Mrs. Crawford was sitting on the front row to direct the angel chorus. The song was a confusion of off-tune *glorias,* but the children sang energetically.

And Mrs. St. Vincent was smiling. Renee fidgeted in her seat and glanced around. Katie wondered what she was thinking.

The narrator continued the story, " 'The shepherds said one to another, Let us now go even unto Bethlehem, and see this thing which is come to pass, which the Lord hath made known unto us. And they came with haste, and found Mary, and Joseph, and the babe lying in a manger.' "

Several shepherds came onstage and walked toward the stable, where they said a few lines and knelt to worship. The angel chorus sang "O Come, All Ye Faithful." Then Mrs. Crawford nodded at Louis, and he took Robbie's hand and marched to the end microphone.

Katie held her breath and looked at the St. Vincents. They were all watching Robbie.

Louis and Robbie began to sing "Away in a Manger." Robbie had a sweet, lisping voice, but it was so small that it could only be heard when Louis was taking a breath. When the two verses of the song were finished, everyone clapped.

Louis grinned and bowed again. Robbie grinned too. Then all the children from the Center came on stage with the boys and sang "We Wish You a Merry Christmas."

At the close of the song, Louis grabbed the microphone, stuck out his stomach, and began to rub it in a circular motion.

"I eat cookies now," he said. "I like cook-ies!"

The audience burst out laughing.

Robbie stepped forward and stuck out his stomach, too. "Yum, yum!"

Katie and Esther smiled at each other in the dark. They both peeked through the crack in the partition and looked at the St. Vincents. Mr. St. Vincent was laughing. And so was Renee. Katie was almost glad that Renee had come.

Then all the children bowed and the lights came back on. The children were free to find their parents and go to the refreshment table.

"Ka-tie, Ka-tie," said Louis, running backstage and peeking around the partition. "Did ya see me? I like cookies. Did ya see me?"

"I sure did, Louis," Katie answered. "And you were very good."

He beamed. "I'm hungry."

"Okay," said Katie. "Let's go eat some cookies." She and Esther each took one of his hands, and they all walked to the refreshment table in the other room. Louis

ran to the front of the line and began heaping bars and cookies into his hands.

"Louis, put them on a napkin," suggested Esther.

"Where's Rrrobbie?" he asked, dribbling crumbs from his open mouth.

Katie pointed to her parents. The Crawfords and the Greshams were standing with Robbie's family at the door. The St. Vincents already had their coats on.

"You must stay for refreshments," Mrs. Crawford was saying. "It's so enjoyable to chat with the children's parents, and I'm sure Robbie would like to stay for a few moments and eat some goodies."

"He really is a sweet little boy," said Mrs. Gresham to the St. Vincents. "And a good little singer."

Mr. St. Vincent smiled. "To tell you the truth, I've never considered that he might like music."

Katie's mother motioned for her to come over and talk to them.

Katie looked out the front window. She felt angry again, and she didn't want to go over and talk to Renee. Every time she saw Renee she thought of all the nasty things Renee had said about her and Louis. It made Katie want to stand on a chair and shout mean things about Renee to everyone in the room. She wanted to yell at Renee for all the times she had said Tracy was fat and Esther was stupid. She wanted to say that Louis was her friend and could come to all her parties, whether Renee liked it or not. She would tell her that the elevator on her town house worked great and that she would never invite Renee over again to play with it. She would never invite Renee over for anything. Never!

Katie looked out at the street. It was black outside, except where the light from the street lamps cast gold beams across the pavement. In the light, Katie could see movement that looked like snow falling.

"Esther, come here," she said.

"Snow!" cried Esther. Louis ran over to see, too.

"All right!" said Louis. "I wanna build snowman. Ka-tie and Es-ther play with me?"

"Sure, we'd be glad to play with you tomorrow," said Esther.

"Katie," Mrs. Crawford called again, "I want you to come here."

Katie walked over to the adults and Renee.

"I wanted you to tell the St. Vincents how Robbie learned to say 'Yum, yum.' "

"Louis taught it to him, I guess," Katie said. "Louis always said 'yum, yum' whenever I read stories to them that said something about food. Louis loves to eat. And Robbie really likes to be read to."

"Well, I thank you and your mother for all your work," said Mrs. St. Vincent.

"It's snowing," said Louis coming up to them. Esther came with him.

Renee glanced toward the window.

"Robbie come to my house and play?" asked Louis, tugging on Mrs. St. Vincent's sleeve.

"When? Tomorrow? I guess that would be fine. Yes, I'm sure he'd like it."

"You play with me," Louis said to Robbie. He led Robbie to the refreshment table. Louis took a chocolate brownie, and Robbie took a yellow, camel-shaped cookie.

Renee pulled Katie aside, leaving Esther to follow them. "Katie, maybe we could go sledding tomorrow at the golf course if there's enough snow," Renee suggested quietly.

Katie was silent.

Renee thought a minute and said, "Esther could even come, if you want."

Katie glanced back at Esther.

"Esther and I are playing with Louis and Robbie tomorrow," said Katie.

Renee's face fell. She watched Louis as he and Robbie walked up to Katie, smiling. Louis put his arm around Katie's shoulders.

"You play in the snow?" said Louis as he looked at Renee.

Renee stepped back, a warm flush spreading over her face.

Then Katie remembered the first day of school, when all the girls had stood on the playground, and Barry Logan had called Louis "retard." And Louis had talked to Renee for the first time. Katie remembered that look on Renee's face—scared, hungry—like a cat in a corner. Renee looked like that now.

"Renee—"said Esther timidly. "You can come over and play with all of us if you want."

Katie, Esther, Louis, and Robbie all stood in a row, watching Renee.

She took a breath and said, "I might come."

It was then that Katie thought Renee was like the little match girl in the story that she had read to Louis. Renee had no real friends. She was alone, truly alone, and she was trying in her own way to reach out to someone. But like Mephibosheth, she needed someone to reach out to her.

Katie took a breath and said hurriedly, "We really would like you to come, Renee. We can play out in the snow with the boys, and when we get tired of that, we can go inside and put on a play for my mom and Mrs. Gresham. And we—we can even play with my town house, if you want."

Renee blushed again, still hesitating.

"I'll invite Tracy and Jillian over, too, if you want," Katie continued. "We could maybe have a Christmas party, with ice-skating on the pond and hot chocolate—"

"Renee, time to go," said Mrs. St. Vincent, coming over with Mrs. Crawford.

"Oh, Katie! That'll be great!" exclaimed Esther excitedly. "Are you coming, Renee? It'll be a lot of fun!"

"Mom, can I have a Christmas party?" Katie asked, snatching her mother's arm. "Can we go skating and sledding and drink hot chocolate and eat Christmas cookies and sing Christmas carols—"

"Katie!" said Mrs. Crawford, laughing. "What are you talking about?"

"A Christmas party! Please, Mom, please!"

"Well, yes—I guess so—if you want—but when? Who are you having over?"

"All my best friends," she said, smiling at the others. "Esther and Louis and Robbie and Renee and Tracy and Jillian. . . ." Katie's sentence trailed off as she looked at Renee.

Renee's green eyes were bright with friendship, and she was smiling the prettiest smile Katie had ever seen.